I0619732

YOLO 6

Sa'id Salaam

Published by Black Ink Publications, 2020.

YOLO 6

First edition. March 20, 2020.

Written by Sa'id Salaam.

YOLO 6

Chapter One

"Pick something," Yolo said when the family entered the basement armory.

"Whoa!" Sun stumbled and leaned against the table for support. "Dad, I feel funny?"

"Got a stiffy, huh, son? Don't worry. Happens to me every time I come down here," Killa said, giving his son a pat on the back. "Come on. Let's find you a thing, too."

"Whatever it is, is gonna be whack cuz he whack," Shyne fussed. She loved being the center of attention and hated sharing the spotlight for even a moment. "Hurry up so I can get back to my husband and baby."

"How about this?" Sun asked, holding a rocket-propelled grenade.

"Yeah, put it in your pocket and let's go. Dummy," Shyne fussed. She was really putting on and her mother knew why.

"You guys have fun. We'll catch you back in the A," Yolo said and guided her pouting daughter towards the door.

"I was looking forward to the flight back. You know, in case your whatchamacallit starts acting up," Killa sighed.

"Why? So you have a reason to take her in the bathroom and give her the business?" Shyne fussed with a hand on her hip.

"Chile, what you know about that?" Yolo shot back.

"Girl, me and my husband been joined the mile high club! One time we—"

"I thought you were taking her somewhere!" Killa said before his daughter recounted a sexual episode that he didn't want to hear about. Her brother thrust his fingers in his ears to keep from hearing it as well. She may have been a married, grown lady, but would always be baby girl and little sister.

1

"You ain't right," Yolo chuckled as she escorted her up and out of the armory.

"I just like watching them squirm!" she laughed when they reached the driveway. They hopped in the rental leaving Sun's car behind.

"Speaking of squirming, we got a stop in Newark. We can fly out from there after we make a slime ball squirm," she said.

The 1-800-Killa app had an urgent request from some terrorized residents of a public housing project. A local gang had lost their damn minds in recent months. Their leader, Chill, went too far by raping a teen whose mother couldn't pay a drug debt. Yolo and Killa were supposed to make a pit stop on the way home, but it was a good opportunity for the mother and daughter to bond. What better way than over a brutal mass murder of dudes in desperate need of dead?

"Grrr," Shyne growled after hearing about the rape. "Dang, I left the Shyne-inerator in Sun's car! This Chill fella needs to feel the heat!"

"Oh, he gonna feel it! He's gonna get the jaza'ah!" Yolo assured her. It sounded good except Shyne didn't know what it meant.

"That's Arabic. What does it mean?" she inquired and turned to face her mom for explanation.

"It is an Arabic word. It means recompense, good or bad. You get what you deserve," she explained as Shyne nodded in agreement.

"The Qur'an says 'there's no reward for good except good' so this dude can expect the worst!"

"And that's exactly what he's going to get!" Yolo replied and mashed the gas.

*****

"Sup, Katie. You got that bread yet?" Chill barked when he saw Kionna's mother traipse through the projects. He hoped she would say no so he could take it out on her daughter once more.

"Chill, Chill. I ain't got nothing right now. I got some money coming tomorrow. My check," she lied. She just sucked several dicks to get money to get high, but had no plans on parting with it, even to save her daughter.

"Say no more. I'll be through later, so make sure Kionna is up," he said, dismissing her.

"Wait! I'll pay you. I just need more time! You can have me!" she pleaded and begged, begged and pleaded, but still didn't come off that bread. She shrugged her shoulders and went upstairs to get high.

"Did you bring dinner?" Kionna asked when her mother came into the apartment. Dinner would be the least she could do after causing her virginity to be taken away.

The savage crack head sold her EBT card for cash for crack on day one. Kionna was forced to eat at school and friends since there was never any food in the house. A few nights back Chill came to collect on her debt and took something she couldn't get back. A girl's first time should be special. Not some brutal thug ripping clothes off, forcing himself inside while smelling like weed and malt liquor. To add insult to injury, her nasty ass mother got more drugs on credit after her daughter's dignity paid the debt.

Kionna could only hope and pray she didn't get pregnant or disease from the incident. The incident was more than she could bear so she hit 1-800-Killa. The site was still up even though rarely responded to. That is until now.

*****

"You ever live in the projects, mommy?" Shyne asked when they reached the rundown housing project. Her turned up face told what she thought about the place.

"Some of these people are better than those rich people out on Long Island. Most are trapped and can't get out," she said feeling for them. The feeling transferred to her daughter who got mad instead of sad.

"And these dick heads wanna make it worse," she said, snarling at the gang members roaming about. They made themselves easy to spot by dressing in their gang colors. Everyone rocked a purple shirt, hat, sneakers or at least a bandana.

"Bet you that's Chill right there," Yolo said when a man stepped out a building, dripping purple from head to toe. It was an easy guess since he was flanked by underlings on each side.

"Well, his chain does say 'Chill' so..." Shyne replied. "How we gone get him? I ain't got time to stake them out for days. Can I just go shoot him in his head so we can go?"

"Too quick, too easy. He's gotta feel what that girl felt," Yolo said, screwing a silencer on a pistol. She handed it to her daughter and did the same to another one for herself. She reached into the back seat and grabbed her bag. "Let's go!"

"Uh oh! Who these bitches?" Chill said when the mother and daughter walked towards them. Yolo was forty something, but could still pass for a twenty something. They looked like sisters instead of parent and child.

"I'on know? But they coming right this way!" Hulk said happily. He wasn't green, but just as big as his namesake. As Chill's right hand man, he got first dibs on whatever crumbs fell from his plate. He just came home from a long bid and got promoted to sidekick.

"You got a lot of sway in them hips," Yolo challenged, unsure of how she felt about it.

"I got it from my mama," she said, making her mama smile. Yolo put a little more sway in her own hips to match. They were bait after all.

"Yo, yo. Where y'all ladies going?" Chill asked, stepping in their path.

"Coming to see my friend, if you don't mind," Shyne snapped sarcastically.

"Shit, I'm tryna be your friend," he said, licking his lips seductively. "She can be my man, Hulk's, friend,"

"Oh, cuz I'm old!" Yolo snapped at getting passed over for her daughter.

"Chill, ma! Not ma like my mom. Like ma cuz we from New York," Shyne rambled, trying to calm her mother.

"Chill, ma," Yolo cut in when she saw the goons looking back and forth between them. She turned to Hulk and batted her eyes. "Sup, papi."

"Chillin'. Sup with you?

"Yo, let's take this upstairs," Chill cut in and turned towards the building. As expected, the three followed him in and got on the elevator.

"Ugh!" Shyne gasped when the strong stench of urine assaulted her nostrils. Yolo knew to hold her breath and the men were immune to it.

"This way," Chill said when the door opened on the 13th floor. He turned and led the way down the hall. A few guys played video games on a huge TV in the living room.

"Y'all niggas beat it!" Hulk barked when he walked in. Yolo gave Shyne the nod and they both pulled their pistols.

"Let 'em stay," Yolo said and fired silent shots that silence them forever.

"What the fuck... did you just do?" Chill asked in disbelief when he processed what just happened.

"Nuh uh," Shyne advised when Hulk flinched. She stepped back and aimed at his face. His next step would be his last. Hulk squinted at her trying to decide if she was really a killer or not. He knew Yolo was since his friend were leaking brain matter on the sofa.

"What's going on?" the leader of two men asked when they came rushing from the rear of the apartment.

"Psst, psst," Shyne replied with two quick headshots and turned the gun back on Hulk. That answered his question as to if she would buss her gun or not.

"That's my baby girl!" Yolo cheered proudly at her handiwork.

"What do you want?" Chill demanded. He was ready to pay whatever so they would leave.

"Justice!" Shyne growled. "Justice for Kionna."

"Yeah, you dish it out, but let's see if you can take it," Yolo said. Chill's face changed since he knew what he did to the teen. He just couldn't find out how she could get justice. He was about to. "You raped that kid and now you're about to get raped."

"I'm saying though, her mom..." he tried to explain, but what's to explained. That was fucked up and he was about to get fucked up for it.

"Raped? That kid?" Hulk almost whined. "Bruh, tell me you didn't rape that girl?"

"Her mother owed me money. Bitch wanna run a debt up smoking my shit, she gotta pay!" he said defiantly.

"And you gonna pay, too!" Shyne said, lifting her pistol to his face.

"Wait!" Yolo shouted, extending his life for a few more minutes. "Both of you strip!"

"Mommy!" Shyne blushed and turned away when the men began to comply. She kept the gun trained on them, but didn't look. Hulk did though and checked out his boss when he got naked.

"Fuck him," Yolo demanded and shocked everyone.

"Mommy!" Chill blushed this time. "Yo, we don't even get down like that!"

"Can we get some KY or Vaseline or..." Hulk said as a large erection began to rise. Now it was Yolo's turn to turn away since she only needed one dick in her life.

"Baby, look in the kitchen for a blue can with a white lid," she said like the late Reverend Cash. Shyne took off while her mother held the men at gunpoint.

"What the fuck you doing? Bruh, I ain't with that shit!" Chill complained while Hulk looked him over. He knew following orders could keep him alive, so he planned to do whatever they said. Not to mention he been wanted to fuck Chill.

"This?" Shyne frowned when she returned with a tub of Crisco shortening.

"I prefer lard, but this'll do," Hulk said, helping himself to a scoop.

"I'm pretty sure I don't need to see this," Shyne said and hit the door. Her mother could handle this while she went in search of Katie. She exited the apartment just as the sounds of penetration began. The high-pitched screams reverberated in the hollow project hallway.

"Oh my!" Yolo blushed once more as Hulk raped the shocked man. Justice is an eye for eye and sometimes an anus and he was getting what his deserved.

"Knew you had some good pussy," Hulk whispered in his boss's ear. He was having so much fun it didn't register when Yolo put her deadly device over his head.

"Chill! Stop, you hurting me," Chill pleaded just like Kionna did when he forced himself on her.

"Shhh, just take the dick," he said softly, just like he did. Hulk picked up his pace when the end was near. Yolo grimaced in disgust when it ended in grunts and kisses on the back of Chill's neck. She had enough and hit the switch.

"The fuck!" Chill screeched again when the big man's big head rolled away. He attempted to remove him from inside of him, but it was not to be.

"Nah, that's how they gonna find you," Yolo growled and aimed her gun. It spit a quiet round right behind his ear and ended his reign of terror.

Shyne had reached Katie's door just as it began to open. Out came Katie looking wild and wide-eyed from taking her last blast. She was already in the hunt for her next.

"Can I hold ten bucks?" she asked Shyne when they came face to face in the hall. She planned to go steal, suck or fuck for a buck, so it didn't hurt to ask.

Chapter Two

"I wonder what mom and Shyne up to?" Sun asked as he and his dad still sorted through the deadly devices in search of his own 'thing'.

"Newark, I bet. They got a head start on us," Killa said, picking up a machete.

"It can be girls verses guys. We'll run circles around them broads!" Sun cheered and raised his hand for a high five, but got left hanging.

"Did you just call your mom a broad?" Killa laughed. It was extra funny to him since he was definitely going to tell Yolo. "Besides it really wouldn't be fair since she has Shyne."

"Word?" Sun said feeling slightly dejected. He shook it off quickly and planned to outdo his crazy sister. Action always did speak louder than words, so he decided to stay quiet and be about that action.

"This might work right here," Killa pondered as he made a few chops in the air with the machete. He knew Sun could wield it like a pro after being trained by Karate Joe.

"A sword, dad? Who am I, Zoro? Want me to ride a horse and carve Z's in people?" he fussed. His father was too busy brainstorming to hear a word he said.

"Come on. We're going to Philly," Killa decided. He grabbed a few guns and cash from the safe.

"What's in Philly?" Sun asked, running behind his father. He would have to wait and see since he didn't respond. A few hours later the father and son reached the city of brotherly love. Killa navigated the city streets until he reached the Germantown section. A few turns later, he pulled up to a house and got out.

"Come on," he said, grabbing the machete and heading up the walk.

"Shyne is gonna clown me until the world ends," Sun moaned under his breath as he followed his father to the door.

"As salaamu alaykum, Habib!" a brother with a large, reddish beard greeted. His eyes went wide with excitement and he his old friend embraced.

"Wa alaykum as salaam, Haneef. This is my son, Sun," Killa introduced.

"Sup, yo," Haneef greeted and gave Sun a pound and man hug. "Come on in."

The father and son entered the apartment and inhaled the sweet Sandlewood burning in the incense holder. A soft Qur'an recitation was playing until Haneef turned it off so they can get down to business.

"What can I do for you?" he said, placing cups of tea before his guest in their Islamic tradition of honoring your guest.

"My son needs a thing," Killa said and pulled the machete.

"Who's he gonna be, Zoro?" Haneef laughed. "Can he ride a horse?"

"Told you," Sun moaned and shook his head. He twisted his lips and shook his head as Killa explained his vision. Haneef poked his bottom lip out and nodded to the idea.

"I have just the thing!" he snapped and took off with the blade. He rushed out to his lab and got to work.

"Who is that dude?" Sun had to ask. Everyone his father knew was somebody who did something.

"That dude is that dude! He's the inventor of the D.C 2000. And Shyne's thing, whatever you call it."

"Shyne-inerator 2000," Sun replied since he knew all to well. It was all he heard the whole ride up from Atlanta. Now all he could do was think of names for his own thing. He couldn't make Zoro cool no matter what he added to it. He let out a deep sigh in defeat and got laughed at by his famous father.

Killa and son nodded off while they waited for Haneef to do his thing. It had been a long 24 hours and it was starting to catch up with them. A couple hours later, Haneef returned with his latest invention.

"Yo, wake up!" he called out and tapped Killa's leg. His gun came out so quick it was like a magic trick.

"My bad. What's up?" Killa said, putting his gun back. The smile on his friends face told him it was good news.

"I bring you... Sun-Shine!" he proclaimed and lifted the machete into the air. Sun just began to twist his lips into a 'yeah right' when Haneef hit the switch.

"Whoa!" Sun cheered in awe when the blade turned white hot.

"I know, right!" Haneef laughed proudly. "It's super hot and electrified!"

"That shit is that shit!" Killa announced. "But my son is kinda clumsy. What's the cool down period?"

"Oh, about..." Haneef paused to turn it off. He counted to two and wrapped his large weathered hand around the blade. "Two seconds."

"Can I see it?" Sun begged and hopped up from the sofa. Haneef handed it over and he did his best Luke Skywalker imitation, swinging the blade.

"Use the force, Sun!" Killa shouted and he hit the switch. An electronic sound filled the air when the blade turned white hot in an instant.

"Yo, pops, we gotta try this out!" Sun pleaded. He couldn't wait to put his thing to good use by killing some bad people.

"Oh, we are. Soon as we get to DC," he nodded. They had a similar request on the 1-800-Killa site. Another gang lost their heads and was about to lose their heads. "What I owe you, akhi?"

"Nothing, I just need you to go across town and handle some deviants for me," Haneef replied with a scowl. "Some clowns pushing that Isis propaganda. I tried talking, reasoning and threatening, but nothing seems to work,"

"Guess me and my son can go have a talk with them," Killa suggested nicely. Everyone in the room knew what that meant. If you want someone to talk, call a politician. Call Killa when niggas need dead. "Fill me in."

Haneef explained how some immigrant sheikh had recently moved to the city. He opened a small mosque and drew attention with his fiery rhetoric. He attracted the young and disenfranchised who didn't read for themselves. He twisted the Qur'an and narrations to bolster his warped ideas about the religion.

Haneef got wind of it and tried to speak with the man. In the end, he concluded that the sheikh wasn't Muslim in the least. That Isis bullshit is so foreign to the religion of peace it wasn't funny. The sheikh recently brought over some of his brothers from his country to wage his twisted version of jihad.

"I thought jihad was to strive against evil?" Sun asked with a pained expression on his face. His best friend and brother-in-law, Asad, was a devout Muslim, so he knew all about Islam.

"And the biggest jihad is against one's own self," Killa added. "People mistranslate it as holy war, but how can war ever be holy?"

"Good question. Perhaps you can ask the sheikh," Haneef smiled. He gave them the address to the mosque built upon lies and deviation then gave his dear friend a hug.

"Until next time," Killa said when they released the embrace. "As salaamu alaykum."

"Wa alaykum as salaam," Haneef said as they parted ways. Killa was pleased at the intensity in his son's face as he followed the turn by turn directions to the so-called mosque. Killa parked at a distance and they watched the comings and goings.

"Hmph," Killa said as a truck from the local BBQ spot pulled up. The place was world renowned, but he never ate there because all they cooked was pork.

"Now I know," Sun said and twisted his lips when the driver made the delivery to the mosque. A foreigner left the mosque and stepped across the street to the corner store. Sun decided to get a closer look. "Stay here"

"Why don't I just stay here?" Killa laughed as he watched his son follow the man into the store.

"Let me have a box of blueberry blunt wraps," the man said, placing a few forty ounce malt liquors on the counter. A sexy north Philly chick walked in and the man stared her up and down instead of lowering his gaze as Islam insists. Sun had seen enough and walked back to the car.

"Stay here. I got this," he told his father and grabbed his thing. The father proudly watched the son enter the bootleg mosque behind the man from the store.

"As salaa... huh?" Sun said as he walked in. He had some slick shit in mind to say ,but lost his train of thought from the sights and sounds. This was supposed to be a house of God, yet it smelled like weed and Bodac yellow played through a speaker. To make matters worse, the sheikh and his students sat around a maidah stuffing themselves with pulled pork and swigging cold brew.

"Are you here for jlihad?" the sheik asked with BBQ sauce on his big beard.

"That's exactly what I'm here for!" he smiled and pulled out the Sun-Shine. A man came from the bathroom and rushed toward Sun from the side. Sun did a 360 spin and lopped his head completely off his body. The head rolled away, but the body ran a few more steps until gravity snatched it to the floor.

"Kill that nigga!" the sheikh demanded and his cronies hopped up. They pulled decorative, yet functional swords from the wall and joined the fight.

"It's on now!" Killa cheered as he watched through the window. Sun hit the button and the blade did what it did.

"Hayah!" a man shouted and swung his sword. Sun simply lifted his and cut right through it. He spun once more and cut the man in half above the waist. The blade illuminated the air as he chopped the men like a sous chef. Soon all that remained was the old sheikh.

"Chill, my nigga. Have a seat. Let's talk about this," he said in perfect English.

"Pulled pork? Beer? Hit the blunt?"

"Nah, I don't want no damn pork or beer!" Sun growled, but he did take the blunt and put it in his pocket. "Now, what's all this Isis shit you been talking?"

"Oh man, I just be playing!" he said and raised his hand for high five. Instead Sun swung the blade and chopped it off.

Sun picked up the severed arm and slapped the man in his mouth so hard BBQ sauce hit the wall. He balled the hand into a fist and commenced to beat him to death with his own hand. Isis if ever there was.

"Now that's justice!" Killa said with a nod from the window. He wasn't the only one watching though.

"Do you see this shit!" a stunned Federal agent asked as he and his partner watched through a monitor.

"I do! That's what I call justice!" he laughed at the beating. "Erase the tape!"

"Malfunction," his partner agreed and deleted the footage. Sun walked right by their van and got into the car with his dad.

"How'd it go?" Killa asked as if he didn't know.

"OK. Let's go home," he said and leaned back in the seat.

"We still gotta stop in DC," Killa reminded and pulled off. He shot a side-glance at his son and knew Yolo and Shyne couldn't hang. It wasn't fair since he had Sun.

Chapter Three

"What the hell are you doing here?" Sun fussed when he awoke to find his twin sitting on his dresser staring down at him. She had that faraway gaze of a lunatic in her eyes and flicking a lighter in her hand. "How did you get in here?"

"Never mind that. I just wanted to make sure you don't punk out on my girl!" Shyne barked. "Oh and you so lucky you ain't have no thot in here with you!"

"I'm telling mom!" Sun whined and rolled over to get his phone.

"I don't care who you tell, punk. She can't save you," she warned and hopped down. Shyne rushed out before he could get their mother on the line. She kept making threats all the way out the front door. "Play with it."

"Crazy ass!" Sun grumbled and got up to lock his door. He still couldn't figure out how she was able to keep breaking in his condo. Instead of calling his mother, he dialed his bride to be.

"Sup, Sun. Everything OK?" Bryonna asked when she took his call.

"Yup, just calling to say good morning," he said, checking his windows, but they were locked tight as well. "What you doing for the day?"

"Shyne and I are supposed to go pick out a dress. Unless... you changed your mind?" she asked and held her breath.

"Never that! I guess we can catch dinner later if you want?"

"I want," she said, smiling through the line. He could hear it and see it which confirmed his decision to wife her. They chatted for a few hours until it was time to get out and meet up with Shyne.

"I can't believe I'm really getting married!" Bryonna sang and did a twirl in her gown.

"I can," Shyne mumbled to herself since she just threatened her brother again. "He don't want these problems."

"I think this is the one," she said, checking herself in the mirror. The tasteful cream colored dressed contrasted perfectly against her brown skin.

"I do believe it is!" Shyne agreed. Now they had to pick out brides-maids dresses.

"I have to go out of town this weekend."

"Work?" she asked since her friend often worked out of town. "Where to this time?"

"Hollywood" Shyne cheered then frowned. "I just hope I can finish quickly and get back to my family.

"I can't believe I'm going to have a family of my own!" she sighed.

"Girl, you've always been family!"

*****

"I have an appointment with Mr. Goldstein," the pretty young lady proudly told the clerk and glanced towards the hotel's restaurant where she was supposed to meet. She couldn't believe her agent got her a sit down with the most powerful producer in the business.

"He asked that you go up to his room," the clerk replied. She felt bad for the girl knowing what waited for her, but she had a choice. She could turn and leave or take her chance upstairs with the predator. The woman had worked here long enough to see a couple of the young girls go upstairs and become stars. She would go up if she had the choice.

"We were supposed to meet for dinner?" she pleaded as if she need-ed help. The woman only shrugged because the choice was hers to make. The elevator door opened and gave fate a nudge.

"Clara?" Goldstein asked when he stepped out and spotted his lat-est prospect. He waddled towards her and threw his chubby arms open.

"Hello, Mr. Goldstein. Oh!" Clara reeled when the man pressed his large body against her. The clerk had to turn away when she saw the horrified look on her face.

"We can go up to my room and talk," he said, shooting a glance down at her pale legs. He licked his thin lips just like he planned to do hers.

"I thought you said dinner?" she pleaded and looked to the clerk who refused to look back.

"I'll order room service," he replied and guided her towards the elevator. Once inside, he inserted his penthouse key for the express ride. He permanently booked to groom his new prospects since his wife wouldn't let him bring them home. Goldstein moved on the girl as soon as the door closed behind them. He reached under her short skirt and palmed her small ass.

"I thought you said you were ordering room service?" she said as she spun away from his grip.

"OK. Yeah, sure," he relented. He knew from experience that one of the expensive meals made it easier to put his dick in them. He snatched the phone off the receiver and relayed her order. She could have gotten a burger anywhere and not had to pay with her dignity.

"So, my agent said you liked my audition," Clara said, trying to direct the conversation back to business. She wanted to be a star and was in the room with the start maker.

"Yeah, yeah. It was good. I liked how you, ummm... yeah, good job," he stammered. All he really remembered from her audition tape was the two big 18-year-old titties in front of him. So close he couldn't help but to reach out and...

"Hey!" she fussed and knocked his hand away. "You grabbed my breast!"

"Look, if you want to get into this business you're gonna have to go along to get along," he explained. Clara had another chance to leave, but chose to stay. She decided to stay and whatever came with it to be a star. Later in life she would join a line of woman talking about how he made unwanted sexual advances. Sure he took plenty of pussy, but most had a choice.

"I'll stay," she relented to his delight. She had a choice and chose to stay.

"Great! Let me jump in the shower," he said, rushing into the bedroom just as room service arrived. "Get that!"

"K," Clara said happily. She once used her vagina to get a ride to the mall, so why not use it to get a Grammy. She snatched the door open ready to tell them to beat it and go jump in the shower. Instead it was her who would be leaving.

"Beat it!" the room service waiter barked. Clara was slow to move, so he grabbed her arm and her bag and shoved them both on the elevator. "He has herpes anyway!"

"I hope you enjoyed your dinner because here comes desert!" Goldstein sang as he came out butt naked. By that time, the waiter took off his hat and he was now a she. A Shyne, to be exact.

"A Tic Tac for dessert?" Shyne asked and cocked her head curiously at the tiny cock.

"Who are you? Where's Clara?" he whined, looking around the suite.

"I sent her home so I could have you all to myself," she replied. That shut up his holler as he checked her out.

"A little brown sugar, huh? You wanna be in a movie? I'll make you famous," he said, rattling off his usual come one.

"I'm more tapioca color and you're the one whose gonna be in a movie," she said, retrieving a camera from under the dome. She pointed it in direction along with the Shyne-inator 2000. "A snuff film."

"Those things don't exist!" he barked defensively. Nowhere near as loud as he barked when she put a spark to him. Shyne aimed at his puny pink penis and spit a ball of fire.

Goldstein ran screaming into the bathroom and frantically tried to get under the shower. However, water only made the white phosphorus and napalm mixture worse. He figured it out when it made the fire spread. He was in so much pain his mouth opened wide to scream, but no sound came out. The scream so too high pitched for human ears, but dogs in the area knew somebody, somewhere was getting fucked up. Shyne took aim at his tonsils and fired again. She kept the live stream of the murder in progress until he was in the past tense. The hundred complainants got their justice by watching him burn.

"Well, Mr. Crispy Man, I have a wedding to attend so..." Shyne explained on her way out the room. "Smelling like bacon, yuck!"

*****

Shyne returned to Atlanta in time to see her brother marry her best friend. The modest wedding was going to be held in a Vegas chapel.

"Uh oh! Honeymoon time!" Shyne cheered and humped the air. "Uh, uh, uh!"

"Uh oh!" Bryonna said in a slight panic. "I almost forgot about that."

"Well you need to remember cuz its about to go down!" Shyne teased. "But don't worry, I'm coming with you."

"Can you?" Bryonna asked eagerly. She'd been a good girl and hung on to her virginity this long she almost forgot it was time to part with it.

"Well, to Vegas I will. You're on your own in your room," she reminded.

The 1-800-Killa site had gotten multiple reports about a rogue prostitute who was ruining lives. Ordinarily no one would care about some John getting jerked by a slimy slut. They deserved to lose everything, but when they found out the woman was knowingly transmitting HIV, they decided to act.

"You ready? Our flight leaves in five hours, so we better get to the airport so we can clear security," Sun said to his new bride. They might make it, but Asad and Shyne were in trouble with Arabic last names.

"No. I mean yes," Bryonna said and took his hand. Shyne and Asad left their son with his grandparents to head out to Vegas, as well.

The two couples managed to get through security in time for their flight despite Asad getting pulled out of line for extra screening. Once their flight got air born, Shyne pulled him out of his seat for some extras, too.

"I need my husband to give me my medicine," she explained to the stewardess.

"I know that's right!" she said after looking Asad up and down. She wouldn't mind a dose herself.

"What medicine?" Bryonna frowned curiously as she watched them urgently rush down the aisle.

"I'll explain when we get to Vegas," he laughed. He fell in love with his lovely bride all over again when she caught on.

"Ooooh. Wow!" Bryonna blushed and giggled shyly. She blushed on Shyne's behalf when they returned. Both she and Asad then fell fast asleep for the rest of the flight.

Chapter Four

"That was absolutely beautiful!" Shyne cheered and wept when her brother and best friend said their 'I do's' and became husband and wife.

"I just wish my mom and dad could have been here," Bryonna sighed. That would be all the mourning she did for people who where still alive and should have been there. Killa and Yolo decided to stay back so the ceremony wouldn't be lopsided. They watched the nuptials via webcam from Atlanta.

"Me, too," Shyne said, but didn't mean it. This was a special occasion, but her and Sun still had work to do. Both would have to find time to ditch their spouses long enough to rid the planet of Dirty Dianna.

The freelance prostitute billed herself as the nastiest bitch on the block and men flocked to book her services. Even family men in town with wives and families still snuck off to have her do things most wives wouldn't and shouldn't do. They paid three times for her services. Once with a credit card on her website. Again when she threatened to send video to spouses and once more when they tested positive for HIV and other party favors.

"Welp, we'll see you guys later," Sun said happily and pulled his new wife from the chapel.

"Remember to breathe!" Shyne called after them in response to the terrified look on Bryonna's face. Once they were gone she turned to tease her husband. "Wanna go gamble? Poker?"

"Yeah right," he chuckled since his wife knew gambling was forbidden in Islam. He knew something that was permissible and pulled her out the chapel, as well. They weren't newly weds anymore, but still acted like they were when they got back to the room.

*****

"Hey!" Shyne giggled when Sun and Bryonna met them for dinner. He was cheesing from ear to ear while she walked with a slight limp.

"Hey, ya'self," she replied and sat gingerly across from her. Meanwhile, Asad and Sun high-fived before perusing the menu. They weren't the only ones going over a menu.

"Let's see..." Mr. Haskins said, scratching his chin as he read the menu in Dirty Dianna's brothel and bar. One side had exotic drink concoctions and the other contained sordid sexual favors. "Golden Shower, Doo-doo Brown, Fist Full of Love."

"We're running a two for one special!" Dianna sang to help him decide. He decided on the three he named since they sounded foreign enough. His prissy wife would never pee on him, shit on him nor ram her fist up is rectum. Like they say, what happens in Vegas stays in Vegas, but she gave them something to take home with them.

Dianna was diagnosed with the deadly virus a year ago, but didn't let it stop or even slow her down. She reasoned that someone gave it to her, so she would spread it far and wide. The blackmail was just a side hustle since she made good money peeing on people.

"Great!" he clapped and followed her to her bedroom. He ignored her whooping cough and entered the plastic covered playroom. Once inside, they stripped and got down to business.

"Right there," Dianna said as she strapped him down to the rotating table. Once he was firmly bound, she climbed up and stood over him and began to pee on him.

"Oh my," he began to protest when hot piss splashed his face. Complaining only made it worse since she peed in his mouth. Luckily he closed it before she began the Doo-doo Brown.

"This is want you wanted!" she reminded as she began to shit on him. She put a large pile on his chest and a smaller one on his forehead. He was fussing up a storm, but she wasn't trying to hear it. He could have stayed with his wife and not get shitted on.

"Now for the Fist Full of Love!"

"No, wait! I'm fine!" he pleaded as she rotated the table. He was now face down, ass up and that can never be good for a man.

"Oh stop whining!" she spat and put on a rubber glove. That was plenty bad enough, but when she made a fist and slathered anal lube on, he had a feeling it was about to get worse. It was and he was about to feel it.

"No! Let me up!" Haskins demanded and squeezed his butt cheeks as tight as he could. It wasn't tight enough to prevent Dianna from punching into his intestines.

"Yeeeeow!"

"I bet!" Dianna giggled and gave him a good fisting if fisting could ever be good. She finished violating him and flipped him back over to violate him some more. For all his screams and howls he still had a raging hard on.

"Shouldn't you put a—" Haskins began to ask for a condom, but she already slipped him inside her slippery inside. He shrugged his shoulders and let her ride away.

"Well, since you... OK then."

Dianna got him off, then herself before climbing down. He breathed heavily and happily, but it wasn't over. The camera was still rolling when the door opened. Haskins got a glimpse of the large man who walked in as she flipped the table back over.

Wh—what, what's going on?" he asked, trying to see what was going on.

"Oh, I decided to throw in a 'Man on Man' for free," she explained when the stranger began to strip. "Well, free for me, but it'll cost you a little more."

He didn't get it, but he got it when the man climbed on his back and gave it to him. The rape tape would cost him a monthly subscription fee of a thousand dollars.

*****

"Where's Asad?" Sun asked in a whisper when he and Shyne met in the hotel lobby.

"Sleep!" she bragged, putting a hand on her hip. "Where's B?"

"Sleep, too," he said just as proudly. Never mind it was the middle of the night and both would have been sleep anyway. That's why the twins decided on 2 AM to go pay Dianna a visit.

"What's in the bag?" she asked, trying to get a peak. She heard he got a thing, but hadn't seen it yet.

"Oh, you'll see soon enough," he nodded arrogantly. They fussed back and forth over who was the bigger hater until a man caught their attention. He was loading cases onto the service elevator instead of the guest elevator.

"Yo, those are gun cases? AR 15!" Shyne said surely. They waited and watched as he came back and forth with more gun cases and boxes.

"Yo, those are ammo boxes," Sun said, recognizing the bullet boxes. This dude is up to no good!"

"Oh he's definitely up to no good," Shyne growled. The man wrapped up his delivery of guns and headed into the casino.

"Well, let's go pay dirty Dianna's nasty ass a visit. She's ruined enough lives. It's time to show her the Sun-shine!" Sun nodded.

"Sun-shine? That is so corny," Shyne teased as she followed her brother out to the rental car. She teased him all the way out to the out of the way brothel. Sun had booked a late night appointment for a 'Trip Around The World' and 'Rock-Em-Sock-Em', whatever that was.

"Let's go," he said when they arrived at the brothel. Shyne followed him out, both having their respective devices.

"Hello," Dianna greeted when she opened the door. Sun cracked a smile at the pretty prostitute and returned the greeting.

"Hey there. I booked an appointment. I brought my wife. Is that's OK?" he said, explaining Shyne's presence.

"She's extra," Dianna informed him since she obviously couldn't blackmail him to his wife if she was here.

"Oh, I'm extra a'ight!" Shyne laughed. Her face morphed into a mask of confusion when she read the menu on the wall. "What the world is a Rock-Em-Sock-Em?"

"Something that'll get your rocks off and knock your socks off at the same time!" she bragged. "Hop on the table."

"Nah, you do it," Shyne demanded and pulled out the Shyne-inerator 2000.

"What the hell is that?" Dianna asked, cocking her head at the strange device. She looked back and forth between the twins and asked, "What the hell is this? A robbery?"

"Nah, we don't want your money. You've been a bad, bad girl," Sun replied.

"Yeah, you been burning men and now you're about to burn," Shyne advised and aimed. She stopped just short of shooting when the door flew open and in stormed her security man or man provider.

"What's going on in here!" he demanded, looking back and forth between Sun and Shyne. He made a move towards Sun and he activated his thing. The Sun-Shine came to life with an electric whirl. The large man swung his large arm and got it chopped off. He looked down at it when Sun swung again and lopped his head completely off.

"Yo! That's dope! Like Luke Skywalker!" Shyne cheered. "Let me try it!"

"No, you never let me use yours!" Sun fussed. They went back and forth about the device and Dianna made a break for it.

"See what you did!" Shyne fussed when the prostitute ran out the back door.

"Me?" Sun reeled in disbelief. They continued to argue until they heard her car start in the driveway. They tore out of the house just as Dianna began to back away.

"I got her!" Shyne said and aimed. She shot a fireball that quickly engulfed the entire car. Dianna hopped out and tried to make a break on foot. A second fireball knocked her off her feet. They basked in the warm glow of the burning woman for a moment before heading back to the hotel.

"Let's go see what that dude is up to," Sun suggested when they returned to the hotel.

"Let's," she agreed. They both headed into the casino and found the man at the black jack table. He sipped whiskey with one hand and played cards with another.

"Looks like he likes brown sugar," Sun noticed when the man eyeballed a young black woman who passed by.

"Brown sugar coming right up!" Shyne said and rushed out of the casino. She hit the elevator and rushed up to her room. She slowed down as she eased into her room. She was relieved to see her husband sleeping soundly. She quietly changed into a skimpy dress and eased back out.

"Hurry up and get over there!" Sun urged when Shyne returned. Their mark was cozying up with a black woman. He bought her a drink and palmed her ass while playing cards.

"I got this!" Shyne insisted and moved in. Sun still never got the attraction to his sister, but watched as she quickly replaced the woman and off she went with the man. He shoved the other woman away in favor of the younger Shyne.

"What's your name, brown sugar?" he asked as he led Shyne towards the elevator. "I'm Larry. One day soon the whole world will know my name. And he you'll be able to say you slept with him!"

"Shyne," she admitted since it didn't matter. "And why will the world know your name?"

The man held his tongue when Sun joined the in the elevator. Sun took note of the floor he pushed and pushed the floor below. Larry waited until Sun stepped off before speaking again.

"You know the big music festival tomorrow? Well, don't go. Stay as far away as possible," he bragged. The elevator opened and he led her down the long hall to his corner room. Sun entered the staircase and ran up one flight just as they reached the room.

"What the hell are you doing with all this?" Shyne exclaimed when she saw the cases of guns and hundreds of clips stacked by the window. She rushed over to the window and looked down on the concert grounds. "What are you doing?"

"I'm gonna be famous is what. Now come on with that sunshine," he said, reaching for her.

"Oh, I got some Sun-Shine for you alright," she said just as they heard a soft tap on the door. She rushed over and let her brother in.

"What the fu...." Sun paused at the huge arsenal of weapons. He quickly raised his gun.

"He's gonna shoot up the music festival!" Shyne told like she was telling a parent on a sibling. She grabbed the Sun-Shine from his other hand and hit the switch.

Larry wasn't the brightest bulb in the box, but knew this wasn't what he had in mind when he brought the girl up to his room. It was time to put them out, so he went for one of his guns.

"Oh no you don't!" Shyne spat and sliced the rifle in half. She swung low and chopped his leg off below his knee. He let out a blood-curdling scream until she rushed forward and shoved the hot metal down his throat and shut him up. "Yo, I gotta get me one of these!"

"Gimme!" Sun fussed and pull ed his device away. "We need to take these guns!"

"Nah, leave them. Let them see what almost happened here," Shyne said. Sun agreed and they both went back to their sleeping spouses.

Chapter Five

"So, how was Vegas?" Yolo sang and rushed to hug her new daughter-in-law. Bryonna was a good girl and she was delighted to have her in the family.

"Painful," she said and winced. Yolo cracked up as they hugged then popped her son on the back of his head.

"Whatever," Sun laughed and grabbed the bags. The family headed out the baggage claim and found Killa parked on the curb. They loaded into the SUV for the ride home.

"How was the trip?" Killa asked when the family loaded into the vehicle. The four all spoke at once as he pulled into traffic.

"Great!" Shyne cheered from the third row with Asad. The newly weds chatted from the middle row with their parents up front.

"Police said they found a man who was planning to shoot up the music festival! It was crazy! He had all these guns! Police were everywhere!" Bryonna said in awe. She was so amazed all that happened in the same hotel they stayed in. What was more amazing is that her husband and sister-in-law did it while she slept.

"Is that right!" Yolo said with feigned enthusiasm. She knew her children had something to do with it the second they saw the news report. They didn't reveal how he was killed, but it had Sun and Shyne written all over it.

"Yeah, crazy," Shyne seconded and snickered. Killa changed the subject and drove them home. Shyne rushed inside to grab her baby from her great grandmothers arms.

"I ain't break him," Diedra fussed and laughed at her checking him over.

"I know. I just miss my little man!" Shyne sang and blew raspberries on the baby's chubby cheeks.

"I'm pretty sure I'm pregnant," Bryonna announced and held her stomach. "Plus, we're gonna have to visit Los Vegas again because I didn't get to see much."

"Besides the ceiling," Shyne snickered. The two good girls high-fived and giggled some more.

Killa did a cook out for his family to welcome them home. After dinner, they all went their separate ways to do the exact same thing. The newly weds went to Sun's condo which they would call home until he bought them a house. Yolo dragged her husband up to their room the second her baby went to sleep.

"So, what's next?" Yolo asked once she and Killa wrapped up round three. She snuggled up on his chest and planted kisses on his goatee.

"Round four if you keep that up," he laughed. He reached for the remote and flipped on the news to see if anyone locally needed dead. They couldn't travel like they use to and appreciated when locals went too far so they could send them even farther.

'Another child was reported missing. This time from Zoo Atlanta...'

"Bae, what's up with all these missing kids!" Yolo popped up and fussed.

"I don't know, but we need to get to the bottom of it!"

*****

'Dear 1-800-Killa, I want to report a conman. He told our congregation we had to pay our way into Heaven. Even had a rent-to-own plan...'

"And I plan to fuck him up!" Shyne vowed and growled as she read the report. She clicked out of the encrypted site and immediately went to book a flight. She'd just booked her trip when Asad came into the room.

"Where to now?" he asked when he saw the travel site on the screen.

"Miami. A church down there has a very nasty virus. The worse of the worse and it needs to be destroyed!" she practically spat.

"Cool. Book a flight for me, too. I'm coming with," he decided. Shyne clapped and complied.

"We can leave the baby with Bryonna and Sun. They need the practice," Shyne reasoned.

"I don't know. Sun called him a da-warf. I'm not even sure what that means?" he asked, scratching his head.

"Well, cuz he's a dummy, but Bryonna will have the baby," Shyne comforted. That was settled, so they made plans for a weekend in Miami. They would see the sights and eat some food while Shyne found a way to murder Pastor Mayes. And boy did he need killing.

*****

"Anyone have any prayer request? Anyone have a testimony?" the pastor asked as the sermon came close to a closing. After prayer request, he would pass the plate, sing a song, pass the plate then pass the plate. American money has the words 'In God We Trust' so more money meant more trust for the perfidious preacher.

"I have a testimony," Sister Esther said softly and stood on shaky legs. The good Lord had definitely been good to her and she wanted to tell all about it. Except pastor looked right over her as if he didn't even see her.

"Brother Jackson?" the pastor said instead. The church 'mm-hmed' and 'yes lawded' as the brother gave his testimony. Once he finished, he overlooked her once again. Time and time again he pretended not to see the lady.

"Pastor Mayes, I'd like to testify and I have a prayer request," Sister Esther said as loud as her tinny little voice could carry.

"Sister, you ain't made a payment in three weeks. Prayer requests are for paying customers. Now, what you need to do is get caught up 'fo yo ass go straight to hell! Hell is free! Heaven cost money!" he said and gave the nod that sent the collection plate around once more.

"Grrr," Shyne snarled as she listened from a rear pew. She heard what she needed to hear to confirm the reports. She eased out during the last song and looked around the parking lot. It wasn't hard to tell the lone Bentley belonged to the flamboyant clergyman. She attached a GPS tracking device to his car and headed back over to the hotel in time for brunch.

"How'd it go?" Asad asked when his wife returned.

"Fine. Almost done. I may have to go out this evening to wrap it up," she said and fixed his buffet plate. Shyne may have been spoiled, but she made sure to spoil her man and child.

"Shukran," he thanked as he accepted his plate. "So, what's up for the day?"

"Same thing as last night," she laughed wickedly. "But after that we can go see some sights."

Shyne rocked her husband to sleep after a day at the beach and evening at a show. She eased out of the bed to shower the sex away then checked the tracking device on her laptop. Her lips twisted by themselves when she saw he was currently at a popular nightclub.

"Good thing I brought my little black dress," Shyne said in a whisper as she slipped into the bathroom. She slipped into the dress, but shook her head at the exposed bra straps. She removed it and marveled at the heavy new breast motherhood made. "Go girl!"

Shyne didn't want to burn up any evidence of the pastor's wrongdoings, so she opted not to bring her deadly device. Better he be exposed in death. She opted to go old school with this one. Biblical even. GPS guided the rental car to the club's valet parking lot.

"Damn shame," Shyne said, shaking her head at the huge aftermarket rims on the car. It was bad enough that he mutilated the car with the big country rims, but using poor, desperate people's money to do it was even worse. She hoisted her heavy purse over her shoulder and walked over to the club.

Being cute allowed her to bypass the long line and join the beautiful people in the shorter VIP line. She eased in with a rapper and his entourage then separated herself once inside. It took a second for her eyes to adjust to the club lights and another few seconds to spot the preacher. He was partially hidden behind a large bottle of champagne and young thot on his lap. The girl wiggled on his erection while he fondled her between sips of bubbly.

Shyne saw her way in when the girl hopped up and made a beeline to the ladies room. She rushed in behind her and followed her into the stall.

"Hey!" the woman complained. Shyne gave her something to complain about and socked her right in her eye.

"Now stay away from my husband!" she shouted for the benefit of the bystanders.

"I'm sorry!" she said and grabbed her eye. She would have a nice shiner in the morning, but she was done for the night. Shyne fixed her clothes and headed over to the preacher.

"Your friend left," she said, pointing at the woman rushing out, holding her eye.

"She got something in her eye."

"I wonder what?" he wondered as he felt his erection slip away. He could clearly see her holding her eye, so what could he do.

"I'on know?" Shyne shrugged. She saw her way in and took it. "She asked if I wanted to go home with you."

"I already paid her though," he fussed at the loss of the church's money. Sure he tricked off with it, but at least wanted to get their money's worth.

"Well, I never charge for my services," she replied honestly. It was her pleasure to kill bad people and never charged a dime.

"Well, let's ride then!" he shouted and stood. The preacher grabbed Shyne by her hand and rushed her from the nightclub. He pressed a tip into the valet's hand when he delivered the pretty Bentley.

"Why thank you," Shyne sang when he held the car door open. She knew he was hoping to get a glimpse of crotch and kept her legs closed tight. She dropped her heavy purse on the floorboard with a thud.

"What you got in that thing!" Pastor Mayes laughed. He liked them young and knew young girls kept all kinds of stuff in their purses. This would be a first though.

"A stone. Well, more like a rock, but same thing," she rambled. She planned to expound once she got to his house.

"Oh," the pastor said and shrugged. He could care less about her rock since he just wanted to lay some pipe. He talked about everything, but God as he drove to his estate just outside of the city. Shyne got even madder when she saw the lavish digs. He was charging for salvation and living like a king. He parked next to a brand new sports car that shined in the driveway.

"I would have got it!" he announced when Shyne opened her own door. She was all for letting a man be a man, but she was eager to get him inside.

"Mmhm," she said and followed him to the door. She braced herself for a grope when he opened the door and stepped aside for her to enter first. Dudes been grabbing booty since middle school, so she knew what to expect. He didn't when she whirled around and slapped him just like she'd been doing since middle school.

"Feisty! I like that!" he exclaimed and touched the welps rising on his cheek. He planned to slap her ass cheeks so they were even as far as he was concerned. "Take your shoes off, please."

"Damn!" Shyne shouted once she took a look around the decked out house. The whole first floor was completely white. White carpet, white leather and tables. Even the fish tank had white rocks and white creatures swimming around.

"Oh, this the white floor. The second floor is all black," he bragged.

"Not for long," Shyne mumbled to herself as he gave her the tour. He was describing the white kitchen as she removed the large rock from her purse. The man had her by several inches and fifty pounds, but she still planned to beat him to death. Stone, that is.

"Ugh!"

"And thi—" he was saying until he was interrupted by getting socked with the rock. The blow knocked him back into the wall. He bounced off of it and was met with another blow to his face.

Shyne shot a knee into his nuts that doubled him over. The next knee dropped him, dazed and confused. Shyne took position above him and stoned him to death.

"Now it's the red floor," she teased the battered corpse. She looked around the now pinkish, red room and smiled. She stripped out of her now red dress and found a bathroom. After rinsing the blood from her body, hair and dress. She put her dress in the dryer and eased upstairs to be nosey.

"Damn!" she repeated when she reached the all black floor. Shiny black laminate floors set the matte black walls off just right. Her search turned up over a hundred grand in cash. She scooped it up to donate back to the church to be put to good use.

Shyne decided she wanted a Bentley coupe as she drove the deceased pastor's back to the club. She parked it and hopped back into her car. She wisely pulled on some jeans and a shirt and pulled off.

"Um, where have you been?" Asad demanded when Shyne returned to the room. He had just woken up to pee and found himself alone in the room.

"Getting this," Shyne said, holding up bags from the waffle joint. Asad twisted his lips dubiously, but he did like waffles.

Chapter Six

"I'm hunting black people. Ug-ug-ug," George said in his best Elmer Fudd impression. He got a good laugh at himself as he patrolled his Tampa neighborhood.

George Gross grew up in the mixed community and got along well with all races. His best friend was black until he came home early and found him knee deep in his woman. He reacted like any man would and jumped on the man. Unfortunately, the man whipped his ass and finished fucking his woman in his face. She added insult to injury by packing up and leaving him high and dry.

A deep-seated hatred of ethnics developed and festered until he took his gun and went hunting one night. His first victim was a gentle giant who was waiting on the bus after work. The cowardly George shot him in his back and ran away. He didn't find out he had made a kill until he watched the news the next morning.

A few nights later, he found a Latino lady walking alone and gunned her down, as well. A week after he killed a mixed autistic man, the police connected the dots. They had a racially motivated serial killer on their hands. They sounded the alarm and went on high alert, but came up dry. Thousands of calls to the hotline didn't yield any leads. One call to 1-800-Killa sent Shyne on her way.

*****

"Mommy, I want a Sun-Shine, too," Shyne pouted to her mother.

"You can save the pouty routine for your father," Yolo laughed. "Besides, that's his people. My people made the Shyne-inerator 2000 that you're turning your button nose up at."

"No, mommy! I love my thing, but have you seen the Sun-Shine? A woman needs more than one way to kill just like she needs more than

34

one purse," she reasoned. Yolo shook her head at the appeal to her vanity.

"Anyway, here comes your father now. Run your games on him because I'm immune to them," she dismissed.

"Hey, daddy!" Shyne said and rushed into her father's arms. Killa melted like he always did when his ladies asked him for anything. "I need a new device."

"Hey, baby. How are you sweetie?" Killa sang while his wife shook her head.

"Give her whatever she wants."

"Sucker," Yolo mumbled to herself. She wouldn't admit it, but she did him the same way. "She didn't even tell you what she wanted!"

"So? I mean, oh. Yeah, what do you need, baby girl?" he asked ready to give it to her.

"I need a Sun-Shine like you got Sun. I'm a girl and girls need electrified, super heated machetes," she said, nodding her head up and down so he would go along with her.

"Oh, that! No," Killa said abruptly. He didn't want to hear his daughter's whining, but it sure beat hearing his son's whine. He released her and left the room.

"Ooh, daddy, my daddy. Girl, stop!" Yolo cracked up at her dejected daughter.

"That's not funny, mommy! They got a serial killer killing minorities and you laughing at me."

"Cuz you funny! Now go down there and punish his ass. Make him feel it!" Yolo demanded. The pep talk pepped the girl up and Shyne lifted her chin.

"You right, mommy. I don't need no dang device!" she said and spun on her heels. Killa returned to the room in time to see her march out.

"Tampa?" he asked since he kept tabs on the site bearing his name, as well. He planned to handle that one himself until she stepped up to take it. Likewise Sun wanted in, but had to go to Dallas to dispatch yet another drug crew who liked to peddle drugs to kids.

"Yup," she replied, knowing him well enough to know what was coming next. She counted in her mind as he processed his idea. *Wait for it. Wait...*

"When's the last time me and her had a daddy-daughter day?" he asked, twisting his lips trying to recall. Yolo twisted hers, too, trying to figure out how he could forget.

"Um, twelfth grade father-daughter dance? You turned the party out. Beat up the basketball team," she reminded him.

"Oh yeah!" he laughed fondly at the fond memory. It wasn't the entire basketball team. Just a few of them who thought it was cool to fondle one of the female students. Luckily, for her virginity, Killa saw them when they drug her out back to run a train on her. He followed them out and beat them so badly they lost the playoffs due to injuries.

"Yeah well, we're about due, no?"

"You're due, yes," she nodded. "Now come on upstairs so I can send you off properly,"

"Yeah and help me sleep on the flight down," he said and followed her shapely shape up the stairs. He wasn't the only one who would be sleeping well on the flight.

*****

"I'm so tired!" Shyne fussed when she and her father boarded the plane. She was still a little salty about being denied a Sun-Shine of her own, but delighted to have her darling dad all to her self.

"Me... too," he said between a deep yawn. He knew why he was sleepy after going three rounds with his wife. "Why you so tired, baby girl?"

"Huh?" she asked instead of revealing she just went three rounds of her own with her husband. "Your grandson is a handful."

"Yeah, he is!" Killa smiled from ear to ear like a proud paw-paw. Both father and daughter were snoring before the plane left the ground. Neither awoke until the touched down in Tampa.

"Thanks for flying with us," the pretty stewardess sang and batted her eyes at Killa.

"Um, don't get fucked up about my daddy," Shyne fussed and put her hand on her hip.

"Oh, I'm sorry," she reeled and left them alone. She wasn't sure if he was her father or daddy but didn't want to get fucked up either way. When given a choice, 9 out of 10 people prefer not to get fucked up.

"You are certainly your mother's child," Killa said, guiding his dangerous daughter off the plane.

"Shole is," she happily bragged. As usual Killa had called ahead and had a car and hotel rooms lined up.

The plan was to verify if he was the culprit tonight and put him on the news in the morning.

"This is nice, daddy," Shyne proclaimed when they reached their suite for the weekend. She quickly ran between the two bedrooms so she could claim the nicer one, but they were identical.

"I'll take the one on the right," he said since he preferred the one on the left.

"That's the one I wanted daddy," Shyne pouted just like he knew she would. She was indeed her mother's daughter.

"OK, baby. Get yourself together so we can go pay old George a visit," he said and entered his room to do the same. Both changed out of their travel clothing and got dressed to kill. They met back in the living room and looked each other over. Both nodded in agreement with the all black everything the other chose to wear.

"Let's ride!' he said and led the way back out to the car.

"What we gonna do about weapons?" Shyne asked as they pulled away. They couldn't bring guns on the flight and had to secure them on the ground.

"I know a guy," he said and kept driving. They reached a quaint suburban house and he led the way to the door.

"Who stays here?" Shyne wondered as he rang the bell. She got her answer when a large man pulled the door opened and smiled broadly at her father. Shyne was always amazed at how many people loved her father. The whole world could love him all they wanted because she knew she occupied the most real estate in his heart.

"Killa!" the pale white man cheered and hugged Killa off of his feet.

"Ralph! Argh," Killa grunted when Ralph squeezed all the air out of his gungs.

"This must be Shyne," he said when he put Killa back on the floor. Shyne took a step back to avoid getting squeezed, but the large man just extended his large hand. "Your father talks about you all the time!"

"He does?" she said, cocking her head at her father while shaking his hand.

"Sure does! Come on in," he said and stepped aside so they could enter. He led the way through the modest house. They entered his basement where he had a display of weapons and deadly devices.

"What's that!" both Killa and Shyne exclaimed and rushed to separate tables. He picked up a tranquilizer gun and nodded at his plan. She picked up a shiny machete and tried to turn it on.

"Awe, man!" she fussed when there was no button to make it heat up like Sun's. She pouted and tossed it back on the table. Both men looked at her strangely then turned to each other.

"Yeah, I'll um, take this. Oh and this," Killa said, holding up the tranquilizer gun for him and a traditional one for his daughter.

"Rent or purchase?" Ralph asked and pulled out a card reader attached to his phone.

"Rent please," he replied and retrieved a debit card. Shyne could only shake her head as they completed the transaction. Only her father had a connect to rent guns. He still had one more connect she would really get a kick out of.

Once the transaction was complete the two killers headed over to George's place.

"Uh oh! I think we're late?" Shyne moaned when they heard gunfire as they reached the target area. Killa, too, feared the worse, but didn't let on. Instead, he mashed the gas towards the suspect's house.

"There's our man!" he growled when he saw a hooded figure walking briskly through the night. The coward had just shot a 60 something year old man in his back as he went to volunteer to feed homeless people. He passed her the tranquilizer and whipped up on the man.

"Psst," Shyne said and got his attention. He turned his face just in time to get shot in it.

"What the—" George griped and went for his own gun, but the strong tranquilizer beat him to it.

"Drive!" Killa barked as he popped the trunk and hopped out. Shyne wasted no time and slid over behind the wheel. He dumped the man in the trunk and closed the lid.

"Where to?" she asked as she sped away. Killa entered the address in the GPS in reply. She wondered why they didn't just murder the man on the spot just like he did his innocent victims. She'd have to wait until they got where they were going to get her answer. One look at the sign above the gate spelled it out plainly. "Eastern Florida Alligator Farm!"

"I told you I know a guy," he said as he pulled into the park. He was met by another man who simply handed him the keys and walked away. He came around and opened the trunk for the guest of honor. "Wake up, Georgie boy."

"Try this!" Shyne offered and doused the sleeping man with her bottled water. He didn't budge, so she went to open the gas tank. "Bet he'll wake up when I set him on fire!"

"Or..." Killa suggested as he pulled him out and dragged him over to the alligator pond. He dunked his face under the murky water until he popped awake. The first thing he saw were a set of beady alligator eyes coming towards him.

"What the—" he asked and scrambled back as far as he could until he ran into the girl with the gun.

"Oh no you don't!" Shyne said, pressing the barrel against his cheek.

"What's this about?" George pleaded like he didn't know. The father and daughter both twisted their lips at him in reply.

"The shootings? But they were... oh..."

"Black?" Killa growled. He pointed the man's own phone at him and pressed a few buttons. "You're alive. Confess your sins!"

George decided he would rather take his chances in court than the girl with the gun or the creatures in the pond behind him. He laid out his plan to randomly kill people of color until he got the man who took his woman. He ran out of words and ran out of time.

"Can I go know?" he asked and who could blame him. He had to try his luck because they might just say, "Sure, go ahead and go".

"Sure. Go ahead and go," Killa agreed. The only thing different was he pointing at the pond instead.

"You might make it that way," Shyne said with a shrug. "You come this way and I'm definitely shooting you."

Chapter Seven

"Thanks for bringing me, baby!" Bryonna cheered when the plane began its descent in Dallas.

"My pleasure!" he shot back since it was still their honeymoon. The key to a happy union is to extend the honeymoon until death does you part. Don't stop doing the things done to get her or him or change into a person he or she doesn't even know.

He came under the guise of expanding his barbershops into franchises so he could kill two birds with one stone. Two birds and a bunch of dope boys who caused a rash of overdoses. One helpless mother just couldn't, wouldn't accept the loss of her daughter lying down. The police wouldn't help, so she hit the 1-800-Killa helpline for support. They immediately dispatch a technician to take care of the problem.

"Mr. and Mrs. Forrest," Sun announced when they reached the hotel desk. He avoided eye contact from the pretty clerk since he only had eyes for his pretty bride.

"You have a package, sir," she said and extended a receipt. He signed for the locked case and turned towards the elevator.

"What exactly is that?" Bryonna asked. She'd seen the case at home, but practiced minding her business like a second language.

"Oh, nothing. Special machete that heats up to a thousand degrees so I can chop up bad people," he said, flashing the killer smile he inherited from his Killa daddy.

"Fine, don't tell me then!" she huffed and crossed her arms over her chest. Sun didn't let the pouty lips go to waste and planted a few kisses on them. They were lucky to make it all the way into the room to do what newly weds do.

"I'm getting ready to make a few runs and scout locations. Wanna ride?" Sun asked even though he knew the answer. His wife was balled up in a fetal position, sucking her thumb and wasn't going anywhere, but asleep.

"Un-uh," she shook her head tersely. Sun gave himself a mental pat on the back and stepped into the bathroom. She was snoring softly by the time he showered and changed. He planted a kiss on her forehead and eased out of the room.

"Well, hello again!" the hotel clerk sang affectionately since Sun was alone.

"Hey," he smiled back at the attention. The smile quickly dissipated when he recalled a verse from the Qur'an Asad had given him when they were kids. He may not have lived it, but read it often enough for it to remind him of itself when situations arose.

Chapter 29 began with 'Do people think they will be left alone and not tested just because they say they believe?'

This was a test of his new marriage and he knew it. The reminder lifted his head in dignity and he tuned her out. Dignity is often mistaken for pride, but they are two separate things. However, dignity is something to be proud of. She twisted her lips and waited someone else to flirt with.

Sun did his homework just like his dad and knew who the dope boys were and where they hung out. In a greedy twist of irony, the local police narcotics squad ran most of the drugs in the city. They got tired of the endless battle that left them dead and dope boys rich. Now you sold for them or you went to jail.

The crew was ran by a white Sergeant who fancied himself after Denzel's character in the movie, *Training Day*. Sergeant Ross ran a collection of wild cowboys known to shoot first and ask questions last. He bought a sports bar named The Wild West to launder his proceeds and personal hang out spot.

Sun parked the rental car in front of the sports bar and scanned the area. In the light of day he planned his escape routes for the dead of night. He did his surveillance of the scene before he turned it into a crime scene.

"Well, hello! Welcome to the Wild West!" a big tittied hostess greeted and gave a shimmy that shook her big titties.

"Those are a test!" Sun fussed at the jiggling breast and rushed inside. The confused woman stood there blinking for a moment trying to figure out what just happened.

He found a spot at the bar and scanned the layout. He took note of doors, windows and exits. It would be easier to catch the crew out in the street one by one but he needed to kill them all at once.

"What can I get you?" the bartender asked, stealing his train of thought.

"Coke, please," he said since wasn't much of a drinker. The man gave a shrug and turned to fill the order. By the time Sun finished his soda he had memorized the layout. He correctly guessed the back room was where the crew held court. It was confirmed when he walked over and tried to enter.

"Can I help you?" a woman asked as Sun tried to enter the room. "Are you looking for Sarge?"

"I am," he decided and nodded. "Is he around?"

"Not until later. The guys will be in this evening," she explained with a smile.

"And so will I," Sun said and turned to leave. He rushed past the titty woman and out to the car.

*****

"So, how'd it go?" Bryonna asked when Sun returned hours later.

"Great! I'm supposed to meet the guys later tonight. We still have time to do whatever you want before though," he offered since he was pretty sure what his newly wed wife wanted. He was right and they stayed in the room doing what newly weds do. They didn't leave again until dinner.

Dinner conversation ran the gamut from God, music, sneakers, politics and food as the best friends chopped it up. Just one of the many benefits of marrying one's best friend. It was all good until Sun looked up and almost choked on his chicken.

"Are you OK!" Bryonna asked ready to perform the Heimlich maneuver on him. She forgot all about him when she looked up and saw what made him choke.

"Shyne! Girl, what are you doing here?"

"We wanted to come hang out since we had so much fun in Vegas!" she explained as she and Asad took a seat at the table. "What's wrong with him?"

"You OK, bruh?" Asad asked and gave him a pat on his back that cleared his throat.

"Yeah. I'm, eh, umm good," he said, glaring at his sister. She got to get the serial killer in Tampa last week, so it was his turn. He couldn't fuss her out about it now I front of their spouses, so it would have to wait.

"You think you're surprised now, just wait," Shyne chuckled wickedly. She stole her friend's attention and let the brothers talk.

Sun excused himself to use the restroom. He shot his sister a glance that told her to follow. A minute later she excused herself, as well, and they met in the hallway.

"What the hell are you doing here!" he growled.

"Dad told me to come help," she said raising her hands helplessly. She knew putting her presence on their father ended the debate.

"I didn't get to go with you and him to Tampa. Me and mom ain't never went on a mission," he moaned and groaned. He knew he had no choice, so he laid out the details of his surveillance. "We gotta figure a way to get them all out of the bar at once?"

"Bruh, we can handle these guys in that back room! We can get in there and give them the business while B and Asad play pool. Unless you scared," she dared, knowing this dog would take the bone.

"Scared! I'm Sun Forrest! Killa's son! Let's get 'em! We gotta get you a silencer," he shot back.

"Oh, I have a lil something. Let's get ready to go," she said coyly and led the way back.

"You OK?" Bryonna fussed over the perturbed look on Sun's face.

"Sure he is. He's Sun Forrest," Shyne teased and cracked up like a crazy woman.

*****

"Be careful. There's a test at the door," Sun warned his brother-in-law as they approached the entrance of the sports bar.

"I see," Asad said seeing the big titties before they reached the door. They were a different set of titties, but big nonetheless. He immediately averted his eyes and ignored them and her.

"Welcome to—" the hostess attempted to greet, but both Sun and Asad sped by.

"You better run," Shyne teased as she and Bryonna came in behind them. They ended up at a pool table with wings and soda.

"What's with the knapsacks?" Bryonna asked when she noticed the twins brought them inside with them.

"Nothing!" Sun and Shyne shot back in unison, making themselves seem guilty. Their spouses shrugged their shoulders since both came to expect the unexplained out of them. They commenced on their gals against girls pool tournament. The losers had to pay the bill and hear about it until the next time.

"There they go," Sun whispered to his sister when he spotted Sergeant Ross and his team saunter through the bar and enter the back room. Both of their eyes went wide when they saw the bags each man carried in hand. Drug proceeds ready to be folded into the bar's legitimate income and dispersed back through payroll checks. At least that was the plan because the twins had plans of their own for the money.

"I have to take this," Shyne said when her phone rang a few minutes later. It was her brother calling from the hall, so she walked off pretending to be on a business call.

"Mmhm, sure. OK..."

Sun and Shyne met at the door and braced themselves to barge in. Once they did, there was no turning back. They had to get in, kill six men and get out in seconds without causing a fuss.

"Check me out," Sun bragged in a whisper and out came the Sun-Shine. He waited to hit the button until they hit the door.

"Check me out," Shyne said and pulled a duplicate Sun-Shine out of her bag. The look on his face was priceless, but she didn't have time to enjoy it. She hit her button and the blade turned white hot before she rushed inside.

"What the—" one of Ross's men tried to say, but a swing of Shyne's blade sent his head tumbling in the air.

Sun has rushed over and sliced a man in half before the first head hit the ground.

"Kill them!" Sergeant Ross instructed and the guns came out. The twins swung and cut the guns in half before they could fire. The next swing took both their heads off, as well. The next man wisely made a run for it, but you need legs to run.

"No, you don't!" Shyne said and cut him off at the ankles. On the way down, Sun stuck his super heated blade straight through his skull.

"Who you calling? The cops?" Sun asked, stopping Ross before he could do just that. He'd just have to figure out a way to explain all the cash because he didn't want any parts of those blades.

"Huh? Nah, I was just... who are you? Who sent you?" he whined. He knew he was about to lose his money, but hoped to keep his head.

"I'm Shyne. This is Sun, my brother. We're from 1-800-Killa. We come to kill you."

"And rob you," Sun added with a nod.

"Shit, you don't have to kill me. You can have the money. I'll get more money," he laughed. "You guys can work for me. I need new men and woman since you fired these guys,"

"Let us think about it," Shyne offered. She and her brother twisted their lips and lifted their heads in thought.

"Nah!" they both chuckled and moved in. A few quick swings turned the man into confetti.

"I'm good?" Sun asked as Shyne looked him over. Luckily for both, the heated blades cut down on blood.

"Yeah, me?" she asked, looking down.

"You cool," he said. They both turned their blades off to put them away. Sun took the money out to the car while Shyne rushed to return to her husband and friend.

"Where's Sun?" Bryonna asked, looking around. She relaxed when she saw him coming back inside the front door.

Chapter Eight

"Dad! Daddy! Pops!" Sun shouted as he barged into his parents' home. He patted his brother and sister on their heads like puppies on his way. Both frowned and knocked his hand off their heads.

"You in trouble!" Yolo giggled. "That's what you get for being so soft. The great Killa, a cream puff around his daughters."

"Am not," Killa lied. He knew good and well it was true.

"Oh, you soft," Grandma Diedra tossed in and chuckled. "You always was soft around the girls."

"Hey, Sun. How was the trip?" Killa asked when his son reached them on the rear deck. The youngest daughter, Diedra, said she wanted a burger and her gangster dad immediately sparked up the grill. But he swore he's not soft on the girls.

"Hey, nothing, pops. Can y'all excuse us?" Sun told his mother and great grandmother.

"We sorry! Let's us get out yo' way so you men folk can talk. A woman ain't got no business 'round men when theys tryna talk!" Yolo said in her Gone With The Wind voice, scrambling to get up. She extended a hand to Grandmother Diedra and helped her up, as well. They both lowered their heads in acquiescence and scurried away. Yolo made sure to pop Sun in the back of his head before they left.

"Bruh, you really didn't see that coming?" Killa laughed at his son rubbing his head.

"Never mind that. Why did you give Shyne my thing?" he whined. "You and mom got y'all thing, Shyne got hers and I had mine. Well, until you give her a knock off version!"

"I know. I don't know what happens when they ask me for stuff," he admitted. "Them girls got me wrapped around their fingers and they know it. I try to be strong but—"

48

"Bruh, you gotta be strong. Learn how to say no sometimes," Sun chastised like he was just a rock himself. He had a date with his wife to see a chick flick tonight that he really didn't want to see.

"I will!" Killa nodded. "From now on I'm telling them chicks no! Hell no. Your moms, that damn Shyne, grandma and that little girl, too. She the worse one!"

"Daddy," little Diedra sang as she and little Killa came out onto the deck. The rule of letting the men talk didn't apply to them. They did whatever they wanted to do.

"What?" Killa barked with his newly found resolve. "Huh? Huh! Huh?"

"We want pizza," she decided even after her request for burgers got patties formed, charcoal lit and her father on the grill.

"Pizza? Girl I—" Killa barked again, but got caught up in her big, brown, batting eyes. The bottom lip poked out and it was a wrap. "OK, baby. What kind?"

"Soft ass," Sun mumbled as his father folded under the pressure and ordered the pizza. "Well, son. I got something for you, too."

"What? A Shyne-inerator 2000 for me? Huh, what you got for me? Buy two cuz Shyne gonna want one too!" he fussed.

"Me and you are going on a trip," he said and watched his son's face light up.

"When? Where? Who?" he shot back, leaving out the why because it didn't matter. Only the worse of the worse got put on their radar, so they deserved what they had coming.

"We're heading to New Orleans. Them niggas tripping!" he growled.

*****

"Y'all kids come on in here now," a grandmother called out desperately when the sun started its lazy descent over the crescent city. Nighttime made the dangerous city even more dangerous when the thugs awoke and came out.

The creeps ran the night, killing, raping and robbing until the sun came up.

"OK, grandma!" the kids called back and rushed inside. Not that inside was much safer. The kids had to sleep in the bathtub to escape the huge bullets from the choppers the thugs favored.

The thugs had held the city hostage long enough. The local police either wouldn't or couldn't handle it, so along came a killer and his son, Sun. Killa literally growled when he read the complaints on his hotline. Babies were dying daily from stray shots and sudden crossfire and it was time to put an end to it.

"But where they getting all this heavy artillery? That's what I wanna know," Sun griped as he gripped the steering wheel. He and his father had plenty heavy artillery of their own, so they had to drive down to New Orleans. It's hard to fly with fingernails clippers, so no way were they getting guns on the plane.

"That's what we're gonna find out!" Killa shot back. He had a good idea since his contacts pointed him in the direction of a local arms dealer. He respected the arms trade, but this particular dealer had an agenda and ulterior motive. That's why he was about to get fucked up and didn't even know it.

*****

"Come on in, Leroy. Wait 'til you see what I got for you today!" Harold cheered as he let the gang leader into his Kenner Louisiana home.

"Sup, my nigga!" Harold greeted despite the fact that Harold was a cracker instead of a nigga. The terms were technically interchangeable since they had more to do with class than color. Not every black person was a nigga anymore than every white person being a cracker. It fit in this case since Leroy was a no good nigga who pumped drugs into his own community and killed his own people to protect his operations.

He was at war with his cousin, Too Tall, from across town. Having the same grandmother didn't stop them from gunning at each other every chance they got. The ghetto kings had enough soldiers to push like pawns in the ongoing war. Each would sacrifice their own queen if need be, but both had love for their sweet Ella Mae Jenkins. Their grandmother didn't try to stop the beef since they both broke bread. Her home was a safe haven with no fighting allowed.

Meanwhile, the mild-mannered gun dealer, Harold, masked his malice behind a meek facade and yellow smile. The same way he hid his face behind a hood when he had on his full KKK regalia. He hated black men with a poisonous passion, but had a passionate penchant for black women. And who could blame him for lusting and longing for the strongest creature in creation? He would have married one if not for his standing as gGand Puba or Wizard or whatever the fuck those people called themselves.

He couldn't pump the drugs that destroyed the ghettos, but supplied all the guns and ammo they could purchase. He was getting rich by supplying both sides of the war. Every time he sold something to Too Tall, Leroy would come the day after the massacre in search of something bigger. They were already running around with fully automatic rifles. Both sides were one step away from bazookas and tanks. Once all the black men were dead or in jail, the black women would be left all alone and weak. It was a page straight out of the Old Testament like when Pharaoh oppressed the people of Moses (peace be upon him).

"What you got for me, wodie? We just got our asses handed to us last night, ya heard," Leroy lamented at the loss of his laymen who were currently laying on slabs in the morgue.

"I didn't hear!" he lied. He knew damn well he saw the news reports of the shooting that left two children dead along with five of Leroy's soldiers. In fact, he sold Too Tall the fully automatic choppers used in the assault.

"Well, I need me some get back. What you got for me?" he said and shopped. He dropped a day's pay on the dealer and left with the same kind of guns used against them plus a couple of grenades. He may have had an advantage on Too Tall and them, but he didn't have shit on Killa.

*****

"So, what's the plan," Killa said instead of asked since it was a rhetorical query. He had the whole assault mapped out.

"Well, kings usually protect their queens, but these dudes ain't got no honor," Sun began. "They do love their grandmother, so she's the key. I'll kill her old ass and that'll bring them both to me."

"Wrong!" Killa said even though that had been his exact plan. "You kill the old lady and that'll bring them to me. Then we get to ride around and clean up the scraps."

"What about this Grand Puba, Fred Flintstone clown?" Sun wanted to know. "If you get to get Leroy and Too Tall then I should get to get him. Fair is fair. It's only right,"

"Paper, rock, scissor!" Killa dared. The father and son had been resolving differences this way since he was a toddler.

"One, two, three!" Sun counted off and they threw. They both threw a rock, scissors and finally paper. The three-way tie only meant one thing.

"Grand Puba is about to get fucked up!" He would have to wait to die since Ella Mae was up first.

*****

"Whoa, lil wodie," Too Tall said as he watched a spectacular blowjob in motion.

It looked as good as it felt, but he wanted to record on his phone for later.

His queen, Amber, let out a gagged giggle since her mouth was full. She was fine as fuck, but didn't have much more than that to offer. She couldn't read, write, add or subtract well, but boy could she suck a dick. Her deep throat allowed her to suck the whole dick instead of playing around the head and using a hand.

"Shit!" he fussed when his phone started ringing. It would have gotten ignored if he didn't see 'Ella Mae' on the screen. He decided to multitask and took the call. "Heyyy, big, mmmm, momma."

"I need you to come 'round here rat now!" Ella Mae fussed and hung up. She knew him well enough to know that he was on his way.

"Well?" Sun demanded while holding the super hot machete over her head.

"He on his way nigga!" she barked and spat at his feet.

"She hot about that dog, yo!" Killa cracked up. Sun split one of her little lap dogs in half when they barged in.

"I'm about to get the other one if this bitch don't get the other one from over here," Sun vowed. No body in the room doubted he would, including the other dog who ducked under the bed.

"I'm finna call Leroy, nigga. And they gonna whoop y'all asses when they get here!" she snarled.

"You won't see it," Sun vowed. He shut up when she called her other grandson.

"I gotta get that," Leroy let out and pulled out of his girl. She recognized his grandmother's ring tone and stayed in place, face down, ass up and waited for him to return. "Hey. Huh? Hello?"

"What's wrong?" Nita asked when he dialed her back. He got the voicemail and rolled off the bed.

"I'on know. My granny said get over there and hung up? Now she not picking up," he complained and got dressed.

"Want me to come?" she volunteered. Luckily for her, he didn't and she got to live another day.

"Nah, keep that thang hot and wet for me," he instructed on his way out of the door.

"He on his way too, nigga," Ella Mae spat once more. Sun had enough of the nasty old lady and swung the blade. He chopped her right in half at the waist. The blade went through her, the bed and got the dog, too.

"Nigga!" she shot once more on her way to the 'Upper Room'.

"Chill, B," the father said when the son lifted the blade again. The woman had left the building. "Save it for Grand Puba."

*****

"What you doing here, nigga!" Leroy demanded when he and Too Tall arrived and parked in front of the house.

"Nanna called me, nigga!" he shot back. Their grandmother called them both nigga since they were in diapers and hadn't let up yet.

"She called me first!" Leroy said and made a dash for the door. Both men competed for her attention and threw mountains of dirty drug money at her, trying to outdo each other. It backfired since Sun went around and collected all the money.

"Me!" Too Tall yelped and took off to the door, as well. The reached the door at the same time and squeezed to enter together. Technically it was a tie, but the man sitting on the sofa with the gun was the clear winner.

"Hey, fellas," Killa sang as if friend, not foe. "Come on in. Close the door."

"Who is you, nigga!" Too Tall barked in hopes to scare the man who gave the boogey man nightmares. Killa lifted his pistol and shot the diamond out of his ear. Obviously that explained it because he put his hand to his ear and nodded, "Oh, OK."

"What y'all doing here?" Leroy asked when Sun came into the room. His tone was a lot calmer since he didn't want his earring shot out. "Where my grandma?"

"In her room," Sun said, leaving out the part about her being in two parts.

"You two have caused a lot of damage in this city. A lot of collateral damage for your beef. It ends here, today," Killa demanded.

"I ain't never making peace with this nigga! Ain't no truce!" Too Tall insisted.

"Hell naw, no truce!" Leroy added defiantly. "This don't end 'til one of us dead!"

"That's exactly what I had in mind. Now fight. Fight to the death. Right here, right now!" Killa insisted and raised his pistol.

"We can't tear our granny house up," Leroy moaned. His cousin stood a full foot over him and he didn't think he could whoop him.

"She not gone say nothing," Sun assured them since he knew dead people don't complain. They have a mean poker face, but never say nothing. That was good enough for him and Leroy took off.

"Ugh!" he grunted and sucker punched Too Tall. The sock rocked the bigger man and he didn't let up. Sun sank down on the sofa next to his pops to watch the fight.

"Damn!" Killa chuckled when Too Tall began to get into the fight. The wrestling match ended up with Leroy in a chokehold. He tried to tap out, but Killa was no referee. He sat there and watched as he blinked death into focus.

"I win!" Too Tall grunted and dropped the limp body to the floor.

"Yeah, but you lose," Killa advised and put a round in the middle of his forehead. He dropped next to his cousin and made it a family affair down at the morgue.

"Well, we got some drive byes to do," Sun said and rose from the sofa. He reached a hand and pulled his pops up.

"Drive bys, walk ups, fall throughs, drop ins," Killa added as they set off from the house.

Chapter Nine

Killa and Sun used the contact list from Leroy and Too Tall's phones to track down their underlings. They had to move fast before word spread and they went into hiding. Luckily, the creeps come out at night and weren't hard to find. True to his word, they did drive bys and walk ups and rid the city of some of its worst citizens. They shot, stabbed, kicked and even strangled the men.

"Well, we better get some sleep," Killa suggested as he choked the last of Too Tall's men into the past tense. He dropped the bad memory to the floor and stepped over him.

"Yeah, let's," Sun agreed. If he wasn't married he would have hit the club for a sample of the city's famous Cajun vagina. He was though, so he went back to the room and called his wife.

"Sucker for love ass," Killa teased and went into his room. He closed the door and called his own wife. Turns out he was a sucker for love, too, but ain't nothing wrong with a man loving his wife.

"Sup, yo," Yolo said, sounding like she had been sleeping. "How'd it go? How's my son?"

"Good. We're halfway there. I'll let you go back to sleep. I'll talk to—"

"No, I'm up," she said and sat up in bed to prove it. "Want me to cum for you?"

"Of course I do," he reeled at the silly question. He got himself comfortable on the bed as she slid her hand between her legs. It didn't take long for her to massage herself to moans and whimpers. A few minutes later, she stifled a screech as she busted a nut.

"Better?"

"Mmmm, better," Yolo said and yawned. "Well, get some sleep, baby. Busy day tomorrow."

"OK, love you," he said and blew a kiss through the line.

"I love you more!" she said and rolled over to sleep.

*****

"Time to pay ole Harold's red neck ass a visit. Time to put a foot up his ass!" Sun said happily as he barely chewed his food. The death toll from last night was over thirty bad people who really needed dead. The city of Nawlins was suddenly safer just that quick.

"Yeah, but don't choke. I ain't tryna hear yo' mom's mouth," Killa warned. "Take ya time. He ain't going no where."

Killa was right, too, because Harold was right at home when they made their way out to Kenner. The father and son scoped out the house and surroundings and formulated a way in and, more importantly, a way out. Killa had sent a text from Leroy's phone to make the introduction so he would be expecting them when they arrived.

"You must be Killa?" Harold said when he opened his door for his guest. It was an easy guess since he didn't have random niggers just ringing his door bell.

"And you must be Harold. This is my son, Sun," he replied minus handshakes. He didn't mind using their real names since Harold wouldn't live long enough to repeat it.

"Walk this way," the host said and led the way. Of course, Killa and Sun mocked the man's peculiar gait. He had lost a leg in desert storm and wore a prosthetic.

"Oh my!" Sun gasped when they reached his showroom. Harold nodded proudly when he saw his reaction.

"I heard last night was pretty busy," he said since he saw the news report of the new record for murders last night. Harold, Leroy and Ella Mae had yet to be discovered and didn't get added to the tally.

"It was," Killa agreed. It was nowhere near his one day record, but fun nonetheless. "You know what? We'll take everything!"

"Every what?" Harold reeled. He wouldn't sell his whole arsenal to any one person no matter what race, but definitely not a black man. "I can't, won't sell you everything!"

"We ain't buying," Sun corrected. He whipped out his gun and expounded. "He said we'll 'take' everything."

Harold was no hoe and made a move for his own hammer. He always kept one cocked, locked and ready to rock when he dealt his deadly wares. Killa was faster on the draw and pulled out a taser. He aimed at his neck and made him do the Harlem Shake when the fifty thousand volts ran through him.

"They always do that," Killa said, shaking his head as the man's bladder released. He quickly reloaded the charge to the taser just in case he had to hit him again. In the meantime, "Strip him."

"Strip what? Who?" Sun frowned. He had no desire to see a naked redneck. The door opened and in rushed Harold's wife with a shotgun.

"What's going on out here!" she demanded. It was a fair question, but she did not like the answer when Killa gave her the same thing he gave her husband. He aimed at her chubby neck and hit her with it.

"Her, too!" Sun whined when the woman peed her pants, as well. "Let me guess, I gotta strip her, too?"

"Yep," he laughed and began collecting all the weapons. Sun let out a deep sigh and followed directions.

"Yo, dude got a wooden leg!" he exclaimed when he snatched Harold's pants off.

"You thinking what I'm thinking?" Killa cracked up as Sun's words over breakfast came back to him.

"Hell yeah!" he laughed and kicked the plastic peg leg away. The husband and wife both stirred awake, naked with black men standing over them. It was a first for him, but she'd been here before.

"Just take it!" Harold's wife screamed and threw her legs wide. She had a better idea and flipped over on her hands and knees and arched her back. "Just get it over with!"

"What are you doing, Ethel!" Harold shouted as his wife anxiously wiggled her ass in anticipation of back shots, She let plenty of black men run through her back in college. After twenty years of short stroking Harold, she was ready to be ran through again.

"They're just gonna take it! Both of them, over and over! Just get it over with!" she pleaded.

"Um, no, we're not," Sun said, looking perplexed. He looked to his father for an explanation, but he didn't know either.

"No, we're not!" he assured her. Killa saw the disappointment in her face and had another idea.

"So, you guys gonna make me suck you guys off? Over and over?" she asked, nodding her head up and down in agreement. She opened her mouth wide and welcomed them inside.

"Un uh," Sun declined, shaking his head vehemently. He backed away like he was afraid of the woman.

"But what you can do is put his foot up his ass," Killa decided.

"Do what!" Harold fussed, but his wife was already going for the peg leg. "What are you doing, Ethel?"

"Just do it so they can go!" she shot back. She was half way right, but in truth she'd been wanting to put the prosthetic up his ass for quite some time. She lost all respect for his hypocrisies of his 'nigga this and nigga that', but always searching for 'black booty' on the computer.

"They're going to kill us anyway!" he shouted.

"He's right, but do it and I'll let you live a little longer," Killa vowed to the Mrs. He held his hand up as if it were a solemn oath. She believed him and moved over her husband.

"Do I have to tase you again?" Killa asked when Harold squirmed and put up a fight. He couldn't blame him since no one wants their own foot shoved up their ass.

"Yes! Yes, you do!" he shot back and got hit again with the voltage. Harold went limp when the current ran through his body. Ethel made her move and shoved the foot where the sun didn't shine.

"Wow!" Ethel remarked when the foot went in a lot easier than expected. A lot easier than it should have. A lot easier than it would have if he was a virgin. Like most racist, he been taking it up the ass.

"He gay!" Sun laughed while screwing a silencer on the tip of a pistol. Harold came to and shook his head at what he knew what was coming.

"That's that bullshit," he griped as Sun took aim. He tried to remove his foot from his ass, but didn't make it. Wherever he was going, he would have a foot in his ass when he got there.

'Psst' the gun whispered and sent Harold off to the afterlife.

"Wait! Just wait!" Ethel insisted when he turned the gun in her direction. "He said I could live a little longer if I put a foot up his ass and I put a foot up his ass!"

"She did," Killa nodded and agreed. He was a man of his word if nothing else.

"Well, what time is it?" Sun asked his pops who looked at his watch.

"Half past a little longer," he replied after a few more seconds ticked off. A second later, Sun aimed and fired.

'Psst' the gun said like a secret and fulfilled their wedding vows of 'til death do them part.

"Now load the car while I search the house," Killa said like a boss. Both set off to complete their task. Sun loaded the guns and ammo while his father collected papers and computers to analyze later. An hour later, they were on their way back to Atlanta.

Chapter Ten

"Look at this! Bruh, look, at this!" Yolo said when she cracked the code to Harold's laptop. She couldn't find words, so she jumped up, spun around and pointed at the screen. Killa rushed over hoping it was some good porn and got pleasantly surprised nonetheless.

"This is good!" Killa salivated and rubbed his hands together greedily. The flyer for the upcoming white supremacist made their mouths water. There would be thousands of redneck, hee-hawing, tobacco spitting, cousin marrying, trailer park dwelling, third grade dropout racist in attendance.

"This will be epic. A family affair!" Yolo cheered. "Gotta let X and Rico get some of this."

"Shit, grandma prolly gone want in on this," he surmised. Surmised correctly because she definitely would want in. "Well, it's a couple months away, so what's next,"

"Well, you and Sun had so much fun down in 'Nawlins, it's time for Shyne and I to do our thing," Yolo sang with that faraway lunatic look in her eyes.

"I hate it for them," he said, shaking his head. The discovery of the clan rally had them both excited, so he reached between her legs to get the party started. That's how it started, but ended an hour later, sweaty, breathless and sleepy.

Yolo called Shyne the next morning with the good news. They'd been waiting on the chance to make another girls trip and some fools in Louisville gave them a reason for a Killa season. Just like New Orleans, the city was overrun with gangs terrorizing the civilians. No one minds a good gang war as long as they're just killing each other. Unfortunately the young thugs can't shoot straight and civilians were dropping like flies. No one made a 1-800-Killa call, but the helpless cries of a mother in mourning on the morning news caught their attention.

"Can I call you back?" Shyne asked from the top of the dining room table. She and her husband decided a table dance went with omelets, so she climbed up to give him one.

"Sure, I'll just go online to buy another crib cuz the way you... hello? Heffa hung up on me!" she reeled.

"Yeah, well," Killa said since there wasn't much to be said. "Can I get a table dance?"

"Can you get a table dance?" she fussed. "We ain't got no table in here, so you gotta settle for the night stand."

Killa cleared the nightstand with his hand to prepare her stage. Yolo took the stand and got to dancing. Dancing led to kissing and rubbing, which lead to bumping and grinding. This time it was Shyne who disturbed the groove when she called her mother back. She got the voicemail when she called, so she loaded the family up and drove out to her parents' house.

"Shyne!" little Diedra and Killa shouted when their big sister entered the house. It wasn't her they wanted though. "Let me see my nephew!"

"Girl, here. Where's mom and dad?" Shyne said and asked as she settled her child with her siblings. Asad stayed near to keep a watchful eye.

"In the room. They ain't came out all morning," little Killa reported.

"Snitches get stitches, little boy," Grandma Diedra warned them as she came out in time to hear the tattletale tattle on his parents. Her mother-in-law suite was directly below the master, so she got the play by play every day.

"What he telling now?" Yolo asked as she came downstairs. "Just like his daddy,"

"Yeah right!" Killa laughed, coming up behind her. His namesake pouted at being called a snitch. "Come on, Asad. Let's take a ride."

"OK, pops," he agreed and scooped up little Killa. They followed him out to the truck for a ride to the store so the women could talk.

"Come help me in the kitchen," Yolo said to separate Shyne from her sister and great grandmother. Diedra had the baby, so Shyne followed her to get briefed on the next trip.

"Please tell me we're going to Kansas!" she pleaded. She recently read a request on the 1-800-Killa site about a serial child molesting doctor. The free clinic was the perfect cover for him to molest and photograph young girls.

"Yeah, I saw that. He'll have to wait until we finish in Louisville. These fools not only killing kids, but corrupting them, as well. Got them joining the gangs in first grade," she replied.

"Oh and they gonna get fucked up, too!" Shyne fussed and nodded. "Anyway, what my daddy up to? Where he take my husband?"

"Probably food shopping. Your brother is bringing his new girlfriend to meet the family," she replied.

"Xavier got another girlfriend? Shoot, daddy may as well get some fast food, cuz he can't keep no girl," Shyne huffed like she wasn't partly to blame. She personally ran half of them away herself.

"Well..." Yolo paused to marinate on it before going on. "Besides you running them off, he picks the wrong type of girls. He's the marrying type, like your dad, but he keeps meeting with these hood rats and party girls."

"You can't turn a hoe into a housewife," Shyne nodded, but her mother shook her head from side to side.

"Marriage turned your hoe twin brother into a husband," she noted and nodded. Shyne had to nod as well because even she saw the instant transformation. She wasn't sure if it was her threats or not, but Sun was being a perfect husband.

"Well, let's hope this Shaqinta, Shanipa, Dominiza, whoever she is, is nice. If not, flame on!" she cheered and pumped her fist.

"Shyne, you can not set your brother's girlfriend on fire," Yolo sighed like any normal mother when advising their daughter not to burn their brother's girlfriends.

*****

"Sup, people," Rico cheered when he entered the house. As usual, he made a beeline to his great grandmother and braced himself for a grandma hug.

"Hey, baby," Diedra squealed and gave him a squeeze. All faces winced when they heard his bones popping and snapping under the pressure.

"He's about to pass out," Yolo warned when his eyes began to flutter. Diedra released her grip and set him down. He wobbled away in search of his father. As usual, the Forrest men folk could be found on the rear deck around the grill.

"Sup, yo," Killa smiled when he saw his son He gave him a pound and hug first and Sun went second.

"So, who this new chick X got?" he asked, looking skeptically.

"I just hope this new one isn't another one of my old ones. That would be awkward," Sun recalled. The brothers usually sent a picture of prospective dates to their brothers to see if they hit her, but not this time. This time X was keeping this one under wraps. Until today that is, the day he introduces her to his entire family.

"This must be serious?" Killa surmised. Asad lowered his head as the deck went silent. The women's loud banter suddenly went silent, as well, and dad had another premonition. "They're here."

"I gotta see her!" Sun declared and marched inside. The rest of the men stayed put for a whole two seconds before rushing inside, as well. Soon the whole Killa clan was in the den staring at Xavier's new girlfriend.

"Hey, guys. Meet Amanda. Amanda, this is my family. Great grandmother Diedra, my dad..." X introduced as he went around the room. Little Killa was last since he was the last one born, but as usual he was the first one to open his little, big mouth. Hence his nickname, Little

Big Mouth. Behind his back, Killa was dubbed Big, Big Mouth since he could talk a blue streak himself at times.

Both parents saw Little Big Mouth's little big mouth began to open from across the room. Time slowed to slow motion like an old school rap video as Yolo moved to cover his mouth from whatever inappropriate thing that came to his little mind. He had adjectives, like fat, stinky, and thot mastered way before he grew a filter for his filthy mouth. A slow motion smile spread on Shyne's face while Bryonna reached to cover her face with her hands.

"She's white?" Killa Junior asked his mom then dad and then Xavier himself. "She's white, you know?"

The little boy was more curious than bigoted since he'd never seen an interracial couple before. Amanda was definitely white by all definitions. She wasn't the sassy white girl who grew up around blacks and sounded black by clipping words or using slang. She was an all American, blue eyed, blonde with a bright smile and golden tan.

"Hello, everyone," she sang and waved. Her bubbly personality broke the ice in an instant and the greetings came pouring in. Killa helped his grandmother to stand so she could get first hug. Yolo followed next, followed by the rest of the family.

"Well, go join your father and them and leave Amanda with us," Yolo said, shooing the men along. Women's talk was no place for men since they would be talking about men.

"Um..." Xavier replied fearfully until his girlfriend shooed him, as well. He knew his sister was rough on chicks he and his brothers brought home.

"Go on, I'm fine," she assured her and followed the women into the large kitchen.

"Bruh, you got a white girl!" Sun exclaimed jubilantly once they reached the deck. "Bruh, you getting white girl head!"

"Humph," Killa said, shaking his head at the fond memory that is white girl head. Color may only be skin deep, but there are some differences whether people admitted it or not. The blacker the berry, the sweeter the juice. Latin women have the hottest vagina on the planet. Chinese pussy is slanted and white girls have thee best head in the world, maybe the universe.

"White girl head," Rico said and his knees buckled. He had to take a seat to gather himself.

"What's wrong with you people?" Asad wondered for the umpteenth time. He'd known them his entire life and still couldn't figure that out. Meanwhile, the Forrest men had a moment of silence for white girl head. Killa removed his fitted cap and placed it over his heart to pay respect. No one will take a knee for white girl head.

"Ugly girls still got that good-good, wet-wet," Sun nodded to set off the debate. No one could argue that because they do. This, too, is a fact. Pretty girls get to be pretty girls with some mediocre middles. The only thing topping an ugly girl is a big girl. So, a big, black, ugly girl is the shit.

"Boy, I had this one so ugly, the pussy gave change! Had gold coins all in my bed the next morning!" Rico announced.

"I had this one ugly chick make a rainbow appear in my bedroom!" X added with a laugh and getting laughs. "Had a pot of gold in my closet when I woke up."

"I had one when I was y'all age who looked like 'Puppy-monkey-baby'. Chick had me fucked all the way up. She had to break up with me cuz I was gone off that P!" Killa sighed. Meanwhile, little Killa looked back and forth between the men and took it all in. He was going to store it all up and repeat it at the most inappropriate time. Probably why he stayed getting his little butt whipped by his mother.

"Come on, Killa. I can't believe they named you that. Let's go ride the four wheeler," Asad suggested to spare both of their ears.

"Wait, I wanna hear this," he declined, but his big brother scooped him up and took him away.

"Yo, we got a mission in a few months. Clan rally, thousands in one spot!" Killa shared. His sons shared a smile at the pleasant news. Racists are shit and were about to get shitted on by the entire Killa family.

Chapter Eleven

"Shoot, now I don't wanna leave!" Shyne chuckled once she and Asad caught their breath from their goodbye session. She planned on being gone a week and got a week's worth of loving in one night.

"Handle your business, baby. I just handled mine," Asad shot back with smug smirk and pretended to pop his collars.

"OK, I don't want you hanging out with my dad and brothers any more," she laughed. The couple cuddled up and fell asleep in the afterglow. The alarm awoke them several hours later. They mentally debated if they should go another round, but Baby Muhammad's mumbles through the baby monitor sent them both to check on him. Shyne did diaper duty while Asad fixed baby cereal. He fed their child while she showered and dressed.

"We need another one," Shyne nodded when she returned to husband and child. "I want them close enough in age to be really close."

"I'm doing my part," he reminded. He pretty much performed on call whenever she came calling. Happy wife, happy life and all, but he liked it as much as she did.

"Well," she said, saying nothing since there was nothing to be said. They traded places so he could shower while she played with their son. An hour later, they were on the way to meet Yolo at the airport.

"Hello, little Muhammad. As salaamu alaykum, my little Muslim man! Who is the greatest? Allah is the greatest!" Yolo cooed with her grandson.

"Awe, look at grandma," Shyne sang at the mother and giggling baby.

"A, yo! How many times I gotta tell you to stop calling me that!" Yolo fussed.

"Just cuz my daughter has a child don't make me no damn grandmother!"

"Yes, it does," Asad said, cocking his head curiously. He was about to explain that was exactly what it meant, but Shyne shook her head. He shrugged and let it go. Yolo wasn't trying to hear that 'grandma' under any circumstances.

"Anyway, you boys have fun. Don't have no women over there while your wife is away," Yolo teased. She got a kick out of her shy son-in-law's blush and giggle.

"You guys have a fun girls trip," he said and kissed his wife and mother-in-law.

Yolo and Shyne boarded their plane for the flight out to Louisville. The thugs had recently dubbed it 'shoot to kill, Louisville' and they were headed to change it back. Neither felt like driving, so they shipped the tools of their trade ahead of them.

"I'm glad you booked first class. Those coach bathrooms are way too small for two people," Shyne said as they settled in their seats.

"Well, first I didn't mind the upgrade since the black glob paid for it. Two, what you mean two people, little girl?" Yolo dared.

"Girl, you too old to understand. You don't know nothing 'bout the mile high club," she giggled.

"You and your brother were conceived in a airplane bathroom," she shot back.

"For real! Nuh uh!" Shyne squealed. She almost went for it until she recalled reading her diary. "Y'all nasty tho!"

"Shole is!" Yolo giggled and leaned back. "Wake me up when we get there."

*****

"Bitch got a fupa," Hot-Rod pointed out as he pointed at the chubby stripper on the stage.

"A what?" his partner, Giant, asked and squinted to see what he saw in the cute girl.

"That lower gut, below her belly, above her box. A fupa. It's an acronym," he explained. He actually had a large vocabulary for a dumb ass.

"A what, what?" he asked twice at another new word. Hot-Rod got a kick out of talking over people's heads. He ran the Diablo Disciples gang in Louisville with an iron fist. Giants iron fist to be exact.

"A fupa. F, U, P, A. Fat upper pussy area," he said, pointing at her gut. He turned his nose up at her and waited for the next stripper.

"Oh, yeah! A fupa!" Giant said as if he knew. His eyes went wide then squinted dangerously when he spotted their target. "Look at it."

"I see him," Hot-Rod nodded when he saw Malcolm and his crew enter the club. He was the leader of the Hell Babies gang from the south side. He spotted them at the same time and pointed them out, as well.

"There that nigga go," he said to his security, A.J. They turned and headed towards them for their scheduled meeting. The recent spate of violence was starting to cost both of them money, so they agreed to sit down and hash it out. The two bodyguards squared off and mean mugged while their bosses gave head nods as greetings.

"Have a seat," Hot-Rod offered and raised his hand for a waitress. The new waitress rushed over to take the order. "Bring them what we drinking."

"Dom P, coming up," she said and switched away. Her shifting ass pressed pause on the conversation until it was out of sight.

"Appreciate the bubbly, but I ain't coming off nare one of my blocks," Malcolm said, cutting through to the chase.

"You don't have to. I realize the fallacy of my prior position and want to make amends," Hot-Rod offered while the waitress poured champagne for the newcomers.

"Yeah, well?" Malcolm frowned since he didn't catch most of the words. He did like champagne, so he and his help picked up their glasses. Hot-Rod extended his glass, so the other three did the same and clinked flutes.

"To our future!" he said and turned his glass up. The followers did the same and all glasses were drained.

"To our future," Malcolm said and refilled his glass. The expensive champagne was free, so he planned to drink it all. Hot-Rod smiled pleasantly as his guest downed the entire bottle.

"Well, actually my future. You guys don't have one," he leaned in and informed with a sly smile.

"Fuck, you me..." Malcolm began, but paused to process the burning inside his body. A.J. burped and grimaced when the sensation hit him, as well.

"Fuck, I mean?" Hot-Rod asked sarcastically. "To my future. You dudes just drank a whole bottle of poisoned champagne. Y'all thought is was Dom P, but it was Jim Jones!"

None of the men were old enough or well informed enough to catch the reference, but it didn't matter. The combination of chemicals in the champagne boiled the men from the inside. Malcolm fell face first on the table and took a forever nap. A.J. keeled over on the floor and died on the spot.

"Let's get out of this dump," Hot-Rod said as he stood. Giant stood to his full height and looked around.

"One second, boss," he said when he spotted who he was looking for. Hot-Rod shook his head as his help rushed over to give Miss Fupa his phone number. He didn't do anything wrong because some of the best pussy on the planet can be found under a Fupa.

"Bruh?" he laughed when his bodyguard returned.

"What?" Giant asked with a shrug.

"Nothing. Let's go to the real spot and look at some real pussy!" he said and led the way out to his car. They headed across town to the Classy Lady lounge. The name was an oxymoron since there wasn't a lady with any class in the whole club.

The men certainly looked better than the beat up broads in the Thot Pocket spot they just left. Hot-Rod planned to bag one of the hot girls, but Giant had a date with a Fupa.

*****

"You have a package for us?" Yolo asked when she and Shyne checked into their hotel. Again they splurged since these trips often paid for themselves when they helped themselves to any money they found.

"Um, no ma'am," the clerk relayed after checking below the counter where packages would be held. Yolo squinted at her, using her human lie detector and ascertained she was telling the truth.

Shyne had a lie detector, too, and checked the tracking number. She twisted her lips to help process the result.

"It says it's still out for delivery with Chad," she said as they headed over to the elevator.

"Hmph," Yolo said, as well. She timed the shipment to meet them since it was filled with deadly devices. She called the carrier to see what was going on.

"Let's see," the lady on the phone said checking the tracking number. "It was just delivered and signed for."

"What?" Shyne asked when she saw the look on her mother's face.

"We got, got!" she growled. They entered the elevator to put their bags down and headed right back out. Yolo navigated the rental car over to the carrier's office and parked.

"He looks like a Chad," Shyne guessed as they watched the trucks return for the day. She hopped out and rushed over to check his nametag. "Damn, Danny."

"I'm sorry?" Danny asked when he saw her disappointment.

"My bad. I was looking for Chad," she explained.

"Figures," he said and pointed at the pretty boy heading over to his pretty car. Both Yolo and Shyne recognized the box he carried and put in his trunk.

"Follow that car!" Shyne fussed. Yolo twisted her lips ruefully at the unnecessary request and pulled off behind him.

Chad had champagne taste, but only made beer money delivering packages. He solved his dilemma by stealing packages from the company. He knew from experience that packages from New York, LA and Atlanta usually contained some good shit. Especially heavy ones like this that was heavily insured. He would just sign for them himself and take them home. The company was on the verge of firing him, but it looks like Shyne was about to beat them to it. Once she recovered her stolen Shyne-inator 2000 from his trunk that is.

Yolo pulled in behind him as he pulled into his apartment complex. They parked near him and watched as he took the box up to his apartment.

"We need a weapon," Shyne said as they hopped out to follow him up.

"Hmph, you might. I don't," her mother huffed indignantly. He had all their weapons in the box, so she planned to use whatever she could find. She balled her hands into hard fist and marched up the stairs and knocked on the door.

"Who banging on my shit like po-po!" Chad fussed and snatched his door open. His scowl dissipated the instant he saw the pretty ladies and invited them in. "Come on in! Weed? Wine?"

"Nah, bruh. We just here for our package," Shyne said, pointing at it on the sofa. There was still hope for him since he hadn't opened it yet.

"That's mine!" he lied, causing both mother and daughter to scan the room for stuff to beat him to death with.

"Listen, I don't wanna knock your hustle, but I want my shit," Yolo demanded.

"You can buy it back then. The insurance gonna pay you anyway, so break me off," he insisted. This was one of those classic 'be careful what you ask for moments'. He wanted to get broke off, but was about to get broke up instead.

"Have it your way," Yolo shrugged and swung. Her hard fist made him stumble backwards a few feet. Shyne stuck her leg out and tripped him up.

"Oh, you bitches done fucked up now!" Chad said as he tried to climb to his feet. However, a barrage of fist and feet prevented him from getting up. "OK, OK! You got it! Take it!"

"I know we got, it!" Yolo said, delivering a few more stomps and kicks while Shyne went to check the box.

"It's good," she called and Yolo put the cap back on the can of 'whoop ass' she opened for him. She held up the D.C. 2000 as well as her own deadly device. She looked around and counted the guns, silencers and bullets to make sure everything was there.

"Bitch!" Chad shouted and tried to attack once Yolo had let up and turned her back.

"Duck!" Shyne yelled as she upped the Shyne-inator. Yolo bent at her waist just as she fired. The ball of fire hit him in his open mouth and exploded. The women grabbed what they came for and rushed from the apartment.

Chapter Twelve

"Where do we start?" Shyne asked, rubbing her hands together like her father always did.

"With breakfast," Yolo replied since they just awoke. She hit the remote to turn the TV on and called for room service. She half listened to the news while ordering breakfast until something caught her ear.

'Another child has went missing from the local. That brings the number of missing children to twenty from the city. Black leaders are calling it a conspiracy, but as we all know, black people think everything is a conspiracy' the anchorwoman chuckled and raised a fist. 'A rally will be held next weekend. Black power!'

"Did sis just raise a fist and say, 'black power'?" Shyne asked in disbelief of what she just saw.

"Girl, yes she did!" Yolo instigated. She heard the ire in her voice and decided to egg it on. "Talm'bout, black people always making conspiracy theories!"

"Well she right about that. Some of these 'stay woke' folks need to take a nap! And all these damn rallies, they don't care nothing about a march or signs or nothing!"

"That's where we come in with that action! They protest cops shooting black people, but never black people shooting other black people," Yolo said, shaking her head.

"That's right and lil Miss Sunshine there is about to get some action," Shyne vowed to her mother's delight. They were here on a mission, but the news reporter was getting beat up on the house.

'On the lighter side of the news, two men were found dead in a local strip club. The cause of death is unknown and who cares! They were black," she laughed and flipped her blonde hair. She chucked up the peace sign and shouted, *'Deuces!'*

"Ooh, mommy. You know I gotta get her!" Shyne pleaded.

"Well, get her then," Yolo shrugged and gave her the green light. "Those two clowns who died last night were on our list anyway, so we'll have extra time."

The girls had a busy day, but started by calling home to check on their families. Shyne was a freak, so she retreated to her bedroom of the two-bedroom suite for phone sex. Yolo called the house phone instead of her husband's cell since he wouldn't know what was going on.

"Hello?" little Diedra fussed in her sassy diva voice. For some reason, she put her hand her hip. Well, where her hip would one day be. Yolo could see the move in her mind and shook her head.

"Hey, baby. How are you? How's your brother, great grandmother and oh yeah, your father?" she asked.

"I'm fabulous, honey. Your son, huh? He is in his country," Diedra said and whipped her hair. Yolo braced herself since anything could come out of that little girl's mouth, but had to ask.

"Huh? What country?" she asked and held her breath. Laughing would only encourage her so she vowed not to laugh, no matter what she said.

"He's from the small country of Urine-nation. Get it, urination. Urine-nation, cuz he peed the bed again!" she explained.

"Get help, little girl. Google a therapist and get help," Yolo pleaded. "Now put him on the phone."

"K, mommy. Love you!" she sang happily and called her brother. "Sheet killer!"

"Hey, mommy!" little Killa sang like a happy little boy when he took the phone. It would have sounded good if she hadn't heard the exchange between him and his sister before he got on the line.

"What did you say to your sister?" Yolo blushed, hearing her baby curse a blue streak.

"You don't wanna know mommy," he assured her, holding up his little hand.

"OK, go wash your mouth out with soap and give your daddy the phone," she advised, holding her breath so not to laugh.

"K, mommy," he said and rushed off to comply. A few minutes later Killa came on the phone.

"Hello?" Killa asked curiously when he saw his son with suds in his mouth.

"Baby, please," Yolo laughed. "Get your kids!"

"K," he said just like the other kids. They ended up having phone sex, too, to start the day.

*****

"Hey, girl," Shyne greeted when she and Yolo met in the living room.

"You ready to have some fun, sis?" she replied. Both were relaxed from busting a good nut and ready to murder something.

"I am. Who's first?" she asked eagerly.

"Let's take care of the help first," Yolo suggested and cut Giant's life span that much shorter. She pulled him up on the laptop and gave a brief briefing about a life they were about to make briefer.

The big man made big mistakes by being too predicable. He kept a regular schedule, which made him easy to get at. Once he was out of the way, Hot-Rod would be easy prey.

"So he'll be at the barbershop at 2," Shyne read from the report.

"Yeah and will meet his daddy, Hot-Rod, around 3 to start their days collections and extortions. So, I'll take the Giant and you can have Hot-Rod."

"No, sis. I'll take the big one and you can have his daddy," Shyne offered.

"Rock, paper, scissors," Yolo announced and got in position. She and Shyne threw for best two out of three and Shyne won.

"Yes, yes, yes!" she cheered and danced around the room. The celebration was cut short because it was time to meet Giant at the barbershop.

Mother and daughter got dressed to kill, but still looked cute. Yolo still looked more like an older sister than a mother and grandmother. Shyne smiled as she watched her mother check her booty in the full-length mirror.

"You go, girl," she complimented as they hit the door. Shyne carried twin 9-millimeter pistols equipped with silencers. She wasn't going to play with a man named Giant.

The radio kept them company on the way over to the barbershop. Both barely listened as they scanned the area. They saw first hand the drama and destruction of the drug damaged city. Teen boys pretending to be men by smoking cigarettes, cursing and carrying guns. The female counterparts dressed like little postitutes while pushing babies in strollers. They competed for the cutest baby daddy with the most expensive tennis shoes. The problem was bigger than Hot-Rod and Giant, but they where about to get fucked up, nonetheless.

*****

"Sup, Giant!" Giant's barber, Nate, cheered like a kiss ass when the large man entered the barbershop. He immediately stopped in the middle of a haircut and shooed the man out of his chair. "Get up. I'll finish you once I'm done with him!"

"Man!" the man fussed as he plopped down in a chair to wait with half a haircut.

"Shut up!" Giant demanded and made the man flinch in front of his son.

"I hate bullies!" Shyne growled as they watched the exchange from binoculars. She reached for the door handle to go kill him on the spot.

"No baby! You can't do it in front of all those witnesses," Yolo warned. "Not without glasses and a wig."

"Thanks, mom," Shyne agreed and adorned the disguise. She pulled her shirt off to reveal a colorful bikini top underneath. The bright colors paled in comparison to the plump caramel breast meat protruding from the top.

"Damn, little girl!" Yolo exclaimed when she looked at her sexy daughter.

"Exactly!" Shyne laughed and got out. She folded her arms behind her back, with a gun in each hand.

The barbershop was buzzing with gossip and banter when the bell above the door rang. Niggas are nosey so all eyes glanced to see who was coming in. They were also in the middle or a war with the Hell Babies, so it was wise to stay on point.

"Damn, little girl!" Giant exclaimed as Shyne entered. He cocked a sly smile as she made a beeline to him.

"Exactly!" she chuckled and upped her guns. She quickly and quietly pumped several shots into his torso.

"Bitch!" he fussed and stood. Shyne took a quick step back and raised both guns to his face.

"Uh oh," Yolo said from the car and reached for the door to go help, but it wasn't needed.

"Sit, yo, big, ass, back, down!" Shyne said, punctuating each word with a slug to his wide face. Giant sat down and dropped dead in the chair. Shyne waved the guns around the shop and made the patrons duck, then made her escape.

"Nice," Yolo complimented when she retuned and pulled away from the murder scene. The public execution was designed to strike terror into the city's gangs. Most signed up for the glitz and glamour. Not to die. The weren't 'bout that life enough to die for it.

"You up next," she replied as they headed back to the hotel to wait for the chance to strike Hot-Rod.

*****

"Damn, ole lady!" Shyne frowned when she saw her mother in her stripper disguise.

"You ain't know?" she chuckled and admired herself. She looked too good to keep to herself and reached for her phone. She handed it to Shyne and turned. "Take a picture."

"Of what?" Shyne reeled and looked at her mother's poked out booty. "You are not about to post no picture booty online!"

"Girl, I am not your great grandmother! These are for your father!" Yolo shot back.

"Oh! OK," Shyne giggled and complied. She snapped off a few poses that her mother shot off to her father. Now that the fun was done, it was time to get down to business.

They rode over to the strip club to give Hot-Rod a taste of his own medicine. No one recognized the new stripper, but she looked like a stripper, so she was able to enter the dressing room. Once she changed into boy shorts and sequined bra top, she set out in search of her prey, but her prey spotted her first.

"Who dat?" Hot-Rod asked the stripper shaking her goods in his face. He always kept an eye out for new talent once he ran through the regulars.

"I'on know," she said and made her butt cheeks clap to keep his attention. Clapping butt cheeks are cool, but not as cool as new booty.

"Go get her. Here," he said, shooing her away with a hundred dollar bill. She sucked her teeth and sulked away.

"That trick want you," she said, squinting at Yolo to figure out who she was.

"Thanks," Yolo said to her and him for making her job easier. She eased up to the VIP section and came face to face with the gang leader.

"You must be new. I never seen you here," he explained when Yolo reached his table.

"I just started. It's my first night," Yolo replied.

"Come on!" Hot-Rod announced and jumped up to his feet. Hers barely touched the ground as he pulled her towards the private rooms.

He tipped the bouncer and snatched her inside. Once inside the room, he reached for her booty.

"That's Killa's!" she advised and slapped his hand away from her backside. "Can we get a drink first?"

"Sure!" he said, eager to do whatever it took to be first inside the new meat. That would give him bragging rights to say 'I hit that first'. He stuck his head out the door and called for a waitress. "Champagne!"

"I got it from here," Yolo advised when the woman returned with the bubbles.

"Now you strip, homeboy."

"OK!" Hot-Rod agreed and began to undress while she poured the glasses.

"One for me, one for you," Yolo sang as she filled the flutes. Of course his got a little something extra.

"To new pussy!" Hot-Rod cheered.

"Or not," she laughed as they clinked glasses and turned the up. "There are several reasons you can't have none. The first being my husband. The last being you're about to die."

"About to wa—" he began to ask before a sharp pain sat him down. He realized in an instant what was going on. "Who sent... you?"

"Oh, no one. This is what we do. Rid the world of people like you," she explained. She watched as the fast acting chemicals did their thing. He left the room before she did.

"OK, bye-bye."

"More than Hot-Rod is having," she laughed and slid into the passenger seat. She cocked her head curiously when she didn't pull off. "Um, what are you waiting on?"

"For you to put on your seatbelt. Just because we're going to do some drive bys doesn't mean we can be reckless," she fussed. Yolo twisted her lips as her own words came back to her from raising the girl.

"Well, how about we save on gas and do some walk ups? Let's kill these clowns up close and personal," she suggested.

"Let's!" Shyne agreed and that's exactly what they did for the rest of the night. By morning, it was Team Forrest 20, bad guys 0.

Chapter Thirteen

'The city of Louisville earned it's nasty new nickname of 'Shoot to Kill' with last night's bloody tally' news reporter, Lily Whitehead reported through her wide smile. She struggled to get through the piece having to pause for fits of laughter.

"This bitch thinks its funny," Shyne growled. She was hot even though she too thought last night was pretty funny. Fun and funny as she and her mother had a blast, blasting the gang bangers into the after-life.

"She does," Yolo said, hyping her up. "Cuz they were all black."

'Police really shouldn't waste their time since the victims were black. I mean they were, black,' she giggled again. 'On to more important matters, a cat was safely removed from a tree...'

"See her earrings?" Yolo said, pointing at the screen. She was observant enough to pick up the unspoken as easily as spoken.

"Cheap plastic rainbows. So what? She racist and cheap," Shyne shrugged.

"And gay. She's a lesbian," she ascertained from the rainbow. Yolo pulled her phone and consulted Google for the answers. "She'll be at clams on the half shell tonight!"

"How you know, ma?" Shyne, asked squinting at the woman on the tv.

"Trust me and dress gay," he mother said, intending to keep it to herself. A glance through the woman's social media timeline was informative.

"OK," she replied and twisted her lips. She said 'OK', but had no idea how to 'dress gay'. Meanwhile she had another pressing question on her mind. "Why clams on the half shell tho?"

"Maybe cuz vagina looks like a clam." Yolo shrugged.

"Not mine!" she shot back definitively, then excused herself to go look. She had enough selfies of her self, but still used a mirror. "Eh, a little."

*****

Later that day, Yolo and Shyne went to the local mall for a little shopping. They always made time to shop when out of town. The effects of the shootings from the night before were immediate and dramatic. Kids, teens and whole families could come out and shop without fear of a wild west, gangland shootout. The only ones ducking and hiding now were the gang bangers.

"I'm going to duck in here to find a present," Yolo said when they reached a jewelry store.

"Aww, something for daddy?" Shyne fawned. Her parents had the best relationship because they were best friends. A far cry from where they started when they were trying to kill each other.

"Girl, stop, I'm getting something from your daddy!" she corrected and switched her booty inside. Shyne spotted a stud and girlfriend walking by and enter a clothing store. She shrugged and followed them inside in search something 'gay' to wear.

"Oh, OK. I can rock that," she told herself when the girl's girlfriend selected a cute, low cut dress. She grabbed one for herself and a pair of shoes to match. Once she was set, she stepped over to the jewelry store with her mother.

"Thank you, baby," Yolo sang and batted her eyes into her screen. Shyne rolled her eyes at the corny display via video chat.

"Anything for you, baby," Killa replied. His bright smiled widened when he saw his daughter come up behind her. "Hey, baby girl!"

"Can I have these, daddy? Plu-leeze!" Shyne pleaded and held up a pair of earrings. Killa opened his mouth to say yes, but Yolo hung up.

"Better call your own husband!" she laughed and paid for her necklace with his card. They headed over to the now peaceful food court and stuffed their faces. Shyne took a nap when they returned to the room since she had a night on the town.

*****

"I must have ate too much?" Shyne fussed as she looked at herself in the new dress. It was her size, but her size was a little tight in the middle. It was too late now to get something else, so she shrugged her shoulders and pressed on. She finished getting cute and stepped out into the main room.

"Sup with your gut?" Yolo asked and twisted her lips as she mentally answered her own question.

"I'on know. Them big ass Cinnamon buns at the mall maybe," she replied and sucked it in.

"Or you're pregnant again," Yolo offered.

"Wouldn't surprise me the way we be getting it in! I be like un, un, uh!" she laughed and humped the air.

"Get help, lil mama," the mother said. They shared a good laugh as they headed out to the car. "What you bring?"

"These," Shyne replied and pulled a pair of shiny brass knuckles. "I'ma make her racist ass feel it!"

"Sucks to be her," Yolo said and shook her head. Lilly Whitehead had a brutal beating on her doorstep and didn't even know it. They headed over to the lesbian bar and Shyne went inside.

"Sup, lil mama?" a stud flirted as soon as she reached the bar. "Buy you a drank?"

"That's past tense you know? It's a drink until it's drank. Then it's drunk," Shyne corrected. She smiled at the confused look on her face then turned away. The stud decided to try easier prey and turned to the next girl.

"Buy you a drunk?" she asked and got another frown. The girl was looking to get drunk, so she nodded and agreed. They copped a few drinks and set off to drink until they were drunk so they could go out to eat. The stud planned on eating a clam once they were.

"Bloody Mary, please," Shyne ordered when the bartender pointed at her.

"A what!" the woman shrieked at the unusual request. No lesbian wants to drink a bloody nothing.

"Coke?" she asked, hoping that was better. It was and she got a nod before the woman turned to retrieve her cola. Shyne was cute enough to attract just as many women as she did men. She was on her tenth 'no' when along came a spider who sat down beside her. "I know you! Your on the news!"

"Lily Whitehead, Channel Five," she said smugly. She didn't like black people in general, but had a thing for black vagina. Who could blame her because the blacker the berry, the sweeter the juice.

"Wow! Your even more pretty in person than on TV!" Shyne fluttered and fawned dramatically. Lily may have been on TV every day, but Shyne was quite the actress herself.

"Do you wanna get out of here? My condo is near," she suggested.

"You take me home and I'm going to make a difference in your life," Shyne said seductively. Lily's panties got moist with the prospect of new vagina.

"Differences are good," she said and slid off the barstool. Shyne followed her out to her Range Rover and winked at her mother. Yolo started the car to follow the truck.

A short drive later, they arrived at an upscale condo building. Lily led her dangerous guest up to her unit and let her inside. Shyne slipped the brass knuckles from her purse and on to her fingers.

"So, you said something about making a difference in my life?" Lily moaned.

"Yeah cuz when you wake up it's gonna be a different time, you'll be in a different place and you're definitely gonna look different."

"Excu—" was all she could get out before Shyne attacked. The first blow ensured she wouldn't be making any more racist remarks anytime soon. Not until they removed the wires from her broken jaw that is. Lily had gotten her ass whipped before and knew just what to do. First, she turned and made a break for it.

"Nuh uh," Shyne said, clipped her feet and down she went. "You gonna take this ass whipping,"

Lily next tried to ball up and deflect the blows with her arms. It worked for a few blows until her forearms broke under the onslaught. She dropped them and got lumps, bumps, bruises and contusions.

"Awe, man," Shyne whined when the woman passed out from the beating. She lost blood, skin and a couple of teeth, but she would live. Shyne stepped over the crumpled racist and exited the condo.

"She good?" Yolo asked when Shyne hopped back into the car.

"Depends on your definition of good. Broken jaw, arms and face good?" she replied.

"Is she breathing?" she wanted to know.

"Yeah and I dialed 911 on my way out," she said. Sirens could be heard in the distance no sooner than the words came out her mouth. "Let's go home."

"One more stop. We got a doctor to see in Kansas before we do," Yolo reminded.

"Oh yeah. Ole doc gone need a doctor once I get hold of him," she hissed.

"Nah, he goona need a mortician," her mother corrected.

*****

"Let's see what we have here," Doctor Cooke said as he walked into the examination room. "Lay back and put your feet in the stirrups."

"But doctor, I have an ear infection," the teen girl complained. She looked over to the nurse who quickly turned her face. She wrapped up the intake paperwork and ducked out the room.

"Yeah, well most ear infections come from an untreated yeast infection. We better take a look," he said and laid her back himself. He came around and marveled at her virginity. He grabbed his phone and snapped off a few pictures for his collection.

"Please stop," she pleaded when he began to molest her, but he wouldn't. She was another notch on his twisted belt. Someone really needed to twist that belt around his neck.

That someone and her mother arrived a day later and set an appointment. Shyne dressed down to look 16 so her mother could get her in to see the doctor. They made sure to be the last clients of the day, so they could be the last clients of his life.

"Shaporiannah Jenkins?" the nurse asked, hoping she got it right. She noticed that the younger the mothers got, the harder the names were to pronounce.

"Here," Shyne called timidly. She got up and followed her into the rear to get her vitals and pee in a cup. Yolo waited in the waiting as the last of the people exited the building. She got up and locked the door behind them.

"Take off all you clothes and put this on," Nurse Adams said, handing Shyne a gown.

"For a sore throat?" she challenged just like she should have. It was a test to see if the woman was as culpable as reported.

"Yes, the doctor needs to give you a full exam," she said, failing the test. A verse from the Qur'an came to mind and put a smile on Shyne's face. 'Whoever intercedes on behalf of good shall share in the reward and whoever intercedes on behalf of evil shall share in the punishment'. Nurse Adams was about to get the same thing the doctor got.

"Hello, young lady," Doctor Cooke sang and smiled as he entered the room. He was delighted to have a new vagina to look at, play in and take pictures of. "Why aren't you undressed?"

"I prefer to kill people fully dressed if you don't mind?" Shyne explained from behind her gun.

"Nurse Adams!" he screamed when the sight of the pistol brought his inner bitch all the way out. He made a move for the door, but it opened before he got there.

"Un uh," Yolo said, shaking her head as she escorted the nurse in at gunpoint.

"Wha—what's going on here?" he asked his nurse, hoping she could explain. She shrugged her shoulders since she couldn't.

"You been taking advantage of kids and now, you're about to be taken advantage of," Yolo said, dropping the bag of tricks with a heavy thud. The doctor and nurse were terrified of the guns, but they should have been more worried about contents of the bag.

"Now you strip and put the gown on!" Shyne demanded and pressed the barrel against his mouth. He quickly complied and reached for the gown.

"Them, too!" Yolo insisted when he tried to leave his tighty whiteys on. Both mother and daughter took a plutonic peek at the pink penis before turning away. "Now in the stirrups."

"You've done this before," Shyne nodded when he quickly hopped on the table and strapped his own ankles down.

"Mmhm," he nodded happily since he had. She came over and strapped his wrist in place as her mother dug into the bag.

"Oh, hell no!" Nurse Adams fussed when a foot long dildoed came out. It was almost as thick as her arm and she wanted no parts of it. "Y'all just gonna have to shoot me!"

Shyne and Yolo both shrugged and shot her so quickly it blew her mind. Blew her mind right out the back of her head and onto the walls. Then turned their attention back to the doctor stretched out before them.

"Lube is in the second door from the bottom," he said eagerly.

"You've done this before?" Shyne had to ask again because he was a little too eager.

"Mmhm!" he nodded once more. He'd been fucked plenty of times but now he was about to get fucked up.

"Oh, you don't get any lube, buddy," Yolo said and pulled out a mallet. It was brutal, but worked with the same principal as lube to get the dildo deep inside him.

"OK, I guess we can give it a yeeeeoooowe!" he screamed when Yolo swung the hammer and impaled him. Shyne took advantage of his open mouth and shoved a second dildo down his throat. She didn't have a mallet, so she gave it a stomp.

"Picture that," Shyne giggled as she snapped pictures of him with his own phone. Then went live to stream his death.

"This, is, what, perverted fucks, like, you, get," Yolo grunted with each swing of the mallet until the stake disappeared inside him.

"Bet you never did that before," Shyne challenged when his rotten soul left his foul body.

"Now, we can go home!" Yolo sighed. "I need some daddy in my life."

"Girl me, too!" Shyne added as they rigged the buildings gas lines. Shyne lit a candle near the door and closed it behind them. By the time the gas reached the open flame, the building would explode. It was another mission accomplished.

Chapter Fourteen

'Dear 1-800- Killa, I hope you're real because I really have a problem. I live in Atlanta Georgia and...'

"Yessss! Local!" Shyne cheered as she read the report. She loved her job and travels, but hated leaving her husband and son behind.

'My boss, Mr Merkel, keeps making unwanted advances. I tried being polite, but it doesn't work. Now, he's threatening my job. I need my job. I have kids. I may just have to give him what he wants. It sucks not being able to have control over my own body...'

Shyne frowned at the anguish she could feel coming through the screen. No woman should have to bargain for her lively hood with her body. She chose to be a clerk not a stripper and should be able to keep her clothes on at work.

"Don't worry, sis. Shyne is on the way," Shyne assured her. Now it was time to do her due diligence to verify the claims.

The 1-800-Killa site was popping, but sometimes it was hypothetical or just plain silly.

'1-800-Killa, come kill my wife so I can have her sister. 1-800-Killa, come kill my partner so I can take over the business. 1-800-Killa, kill my publisher because they won't pay me. 1-800-Killa this bitch keep liking my man's pictures. My neighbor took my shovel, blah, blah, blah.'

Everybody had somebody they wanted dead.

"On the way where?" Asad asked as he walked in on her conversation.

"On my way to rock your world!" she said, closing the laptop. Asad twisted his lips as a dare knowing she loved a good dare. They met in the middle of their bed and got to rocking. In the end, both got rocked to sleep.

*****

Janice pulled up to the rendezvous spot and parked. She arrived early, so she would have time to break down and cry. That's exactly what she did when she read the sign above the motel. She'd never been a cheap woman, but here she was at the cheap hotel ready to sleep with her boss in the cheap suites. She needed her meager salary, but health insurance for her kids, as well. She had always provided for her three children without help, but she needed help now.

"Janice?" Mr. Merkel asked and tapped on her car window. She looked startled at her watch not realizing she had been here that long.

"Yeah. Hey, um, Mr. Merkel," she stammered and got out of the car.

"Call me Henry. For now cuz once we get inside, you're gonna wanna call me daddy!" he said greedily gobbling her body with his beady eyes. He was ugly in the office but even more so in the light of day.

She looked down at his large booty in the cheap polyester slacks as he led the way to the room. He opened the door and stepped aside so she could enter. The pungent aroma of the previous people's sex still lingered in the air. Years of smoke and alcohol was trapped in the heavy curtains and threatened to make her lose her lunch.

"You OK?" he asked, seeing her wretch from the odor. Most women did that around him and he had yet to figure out why. Gross people are usually the last to know how gross they really are.

"No, I mean, yes," she said, backing out and backing back in, in an instant. "Come on. Let's get on with it."

"Can't wait, huh!" he cheered himself on. Again most women seemed to be in a rush when he got them here. Little did he know, they just wanted to get it over with. If this is what it took to keep food on the table, they just wanted to do it and put it behind them.

"You said just once. One time," she reminded him of their deal. "And I get to keep my job."

"Sure, sure. Keep your job," he blurted out and began to undress. Janice turned her head to avoid the pale, lumpy man in front of her. She quickly stripped down to the suite she wore on her first birthday and slid under the cigarette-smelling comforter.

"Let's start with a little appetizer," Merkel suggested as he slid between her legs. Janice actually anticipated a little head since she hadn't had any in some time. Being a single parent consumes a lot of time. Being a good one required even more time, which left no time for dating.

"Ow!" she fussed when he nibbled on her labia. "Could you please just lick? Yeah, that's better."

Actually, it wasn't better. It just didn't hurt. It didn't feel good either as he licked and slobbered between her legs. A gross wetness pooled under her from his own saliva.

"This thing is all wet!!" he cheered triumphantly as he came face to face with her. She turned hers just in time to miss getting slobbered on her mouth. He'd left enough spit on one set of lips already. "Ready for this wood?"

"Yeah, sure," Janice agreed as he worked himself inside of her. His average sized penis would have probably felt good if this was fully consensual. It was actually rape by default because she had no choice.

"Shit," Janice fussed at herself for feeling good. She was repulsed at being here with him inside of her, but damn if he didn't feel good inside of her. She made a mental decision to cum so it wouldn't be a total loss. It had been so long since she....

"Ugh, argh, shit, whew!" he grumbled and groaned as it came to an abrupt end. She realized what was happening and shoved him out of her just before he began spewing globs of semen on her belly. She grimaced at the sight and feel of warm baby batter, but better on her than in her. "Round two?"

"Um, no! We had a deal. You got what you wanted and I get to keep my job," she said forcefully.

"Yeah, but you still need hours, don't you? I mean, you do have kids to feed," he reminded. It reminded her just why she made the complaint to 1-800-Killa in the first place.

Janice let out a deep sigh as she let her bastard boss back inside of her. He humped and thrashed, moaned and humped his way to yet another nut and deposited on her stomach with the last one. Now all she had to do was meet him once a week so she could keep her hours.

*****

Shyne set up an interview a few days later for an opening at the call center. She was delighted to have Mr. Merkel himself do the interview. She made sure to dress modestly so it couldn't be said she enticed inappropriate comments. Not to mention her husband wouldn't let her leave the house any other way. Shyne had plenty of daisy dukes and mini skirts to wear around the house, but always guarded her modesty outside of it.

"Susan Jennings?" Mr. Merkel asked and extended his hand as he entered the interview room. Shyne frowned at the strange name until she remembered using it on the resume she submitted.

"Yes, nice to meet you," she greeted in return and stood to shake his hand. She almost pulled away from his clammy hand when he gave her a terse shake designed to shake her breast. He locked in on her blouse to see what she was working with.

"Reviewing your resume and, um, we really have a ton of interest in the position," he said similar to how and why a spider spins a web.

"I really am eager to work here. I'm a fast learner and have a great work ethic," she explained quite professionally.

"Well, what sets you apart from the other applicants? What positions are you willing to do for the position?" he asked and winked.

"Explain exactly what do you mean?" Shyne dared and blinked like a girly girl.

"69? Reverse cowgirl? What's your favorite? Mines is 69, AKA the best of both worlds," he said as seductively as a pudgy, pale, 55 year old man can. Shyne drifted in her own head at the best of both worlds statement. There were so many things she and her husband had yet to try. "Hello?"

"My bad. So, you're saying that if I sleep with you I can have the job?" she asked plainly.

"That's exactly what I'm saying. And you can get all the extra hours you like," he laid out.

"OK," Shyne agreed since she was spinning a web of her own. She jotted down and address and pushed it across the desk. "Meet me here. Nine o'clock?"

"And by 9:30, you'll be in love," he said, flattering no one but himself. He wouldn't last until 9:05 if he made the meeting.

*****

"Eenie, meenie, minie... mo," Shyne sang as she sorted through her and her brothers growing arsenal. It was nothing like their parents, but deadly nonetheless. Their twin machetes hung side by side looking just like them. They had the perfect name of Sun-Shine for Sun and Shyne. "Nah, need something to make him suffer."

The machetes put victims in shock from seeing their arms and legs rolling away. The DC 2000 was too quick and actually painless. The Shyne-inator 2000 ended up getting the call once again.

Shyne headed across town to cheap motel for her date with the sex bully. The rundown spot was a mecca for crack heads, so they were used to fires. Mr. Merkel was so excited about the pretty, young girl he arrived early. He was used to the thirty something single moms who desperately needed their jobs.

"Hey, there!" he cheered when Shyne pulled up next to him. "I would have gotten us a room somewhere better."

"Oh, this is just fine for what I had in mind," she explained and used a key to enter one of the rooms.

"Smells like gas," he said, sniffing the air as they entered.

"Oh, that's probably just me," she said since she had to fuel up her deadly device. The device was like a paint ball on steroids that spit out a napalm like substance.

"Well, let's get comfortable," he suggested and motioned towards the bed.

"How's about a shower first?" Shyne suggested and entered the bathroom. Merkel rushed in behind her and quickly stripped out of his clothes. Meanwhile, Shyne removed some items from her bag. The first being a pair of handcuffs.

"Kinky, I see!" he cheered and got a stiffy.

"Yup, and I'm gonna set your dick on fire!" she vowed as she cuffed one wrist to the shower curtain.

"Sounds hot!" he said figuratively, unaware she meant literally. He tilted his head curiously when the Shyne-inator 2000 came into view. "What's that?"

"I'm glad you asked. I'll let it explain," she said and took a step back. She fired her fire gun at his midsection and it went up in flames.

"Um?" Mr. Merkel asked, trying to reconcile what was happening. Then the intense pain of the intense flames began to register. He reached for the faucet to douse the fire but it only made it worse.

"This is how your victims felt!" Shyne said. She had to shout over his howls and screams. He missed most of the admonishment from the pain of the punishment. Shyne pulled out a silencer-equipped pistol and fired a round into his thigh. A spurt of arterial blood told her she hit her mark. He would burn and bleed out at the same time, so she turned and left him to his misery.

"OK, bye-bye!"

*****

"Girl, you gotta get your own tag line!" Yolo fussed and interrupted as her daughter filled her in about the latest hit. "I need to trademark 'OK, bye-bye.'"

"You can't trademark that!" Shyne giggled, but she knew her mother was right.

"How 'bout 'see ya, I wouldn't wanna be ya!" Shyne cheered while Yolo twisted her lips. "Or 'Rockabye baby!' Huh? Dope, ain't it!"

"I'm gonna need you to not watch New Jack City anymore. Please and thank you," she said.

"But mama, it be calling me! I can't shake it. I just cain't!" Shyne said in her best Pookie voice.

"Anyway, look at this latest request on the site. It's from Los Angeles. Tell me who it sounds like," Yolo said, turning her laptop to face Shyne.

"Let's see here..." Shyne said and began to read.

'Dear 1-800-Killa. I feel silly but, I need to vent. I'm a doctor in LA and I just opened my own clinic, which is great for a girl from Wyandanch...'

"Wyandanch!" Shyne shrieked seeing their hometown. The other similarities had yet to register.

"Keep reading, little mama," her mother urged and rocked her grandson.

'I try to provide quality care for the people, but the insurance company keeps rejecting the claims. I spoke to the rep, a clown named Art Pence and he said if people can't afford medical care, they shouldn't get sick! Meanwhile he's tooling around town in a Bentley. It would be just awesome sauce if you could come kill him. A really, really brutal death.'

"Awesome sauce? Wyandanch? That sounds like... Christi!" Shyne finally caught on. "I just spoke to her yesterday and she said everything was great!"

"Well, she does try to stay positive. Keep reading," Yolo said and scrolled to the next complaint.

'Oh yeah, while I'm at it, I have a young patient who lives alone with her dad and is on her third child. She's 17 with three children and a father who hovers over her even during exams. She never speaks and never

smiles. Something isn't right. It would be cool if you killed him, too. OK, thank you'.

"You sure she's adopted? Cuz she kinda sounds like us," Shyne chuckled.

"Adopted or not, she's a Forrest. You know what's up now, don't you?" Yolo asked with a sly smile.

"Looks like I'm headed to Cali" Shyne cheered eagerly. She'd been meaning to get out to see her big sister again and now had the chance.

"Looks like we're..." Yolo said, pausing to point between herself and her daughter, "Going to Cali."

"Well, let's bring our men cuz I can't go that long without no di—um, man," Shyne said.

"You are your mother's daughter," Yolo nodded. She didn't like going days without her man and his man either. Looks like they were all headed to sunny California

Chapter Fifteen

"You lucky my mom and dad are here cuz I'd take you in that bathroom and rock yo' world!" Shyne threatened once the sign came on to unfasten seatbelts. It wouldn't be the first time so he took the threat as a promise.

"That bathroom?" Asad asked, pointing to Killa and Yolo entering the plane's bathroom together.

"They are too much. Just do it anywhere. Just nasty," she fussed. Her husband just squinted at the little hypocrite but didn't say a word. "Oh, be quiet."

"Yeah, I know," he laughed, causing their baby to laugh and show off his one tooth.

"Come on with it!" Killa urged when he and Yolo closed the bathroom door. He sat on the closed commode while she hiked her long dress up above her waist. No panties meant it was chow time. She kicked a leg high in the air like a ballerina and rested on the wall.

"Sssss," she hissed when he began to kiss and lick. He twirled his tongue around her clit and darted it in and out her slippery slope. She gripped the handles on the wall to keep from floating away. Either the plane flew through some turbulence or Yolo came hard enough to shake the cabin. "Mmm, now you come on with it!"

"One heaping helping of dick coming up," he said and stood. Yolo licked and kissed her own juice from his mouth then sucked it off his tongue while he nestled inside of her. She wrapped her legs around his back and let him get it. He got it too, every bit of it.

"Here, we... sss, go again," she moaned as a second nut crept into her life. She shivered and shook once again, but this time he shook with her.

"Whooo Weeee!" he exclaimed as he pulsed and throbbed in ecstasy. Once they got themselves cleaned up they eased out like nothing happened.

"Mmhm," Shyne said, twisting her mother and father when they took their seats.

"Don't be a hater, lil girl," Yolo teased. She and Killa were both sleep in seconds. They woke up halfway across the country and went back into the bathroom for seconds.

*****

"Mom, Dad!" Christi cheered lovingly when she spotted Killa and Yolo as they made their way to the baggage claim. She saw her little sister and lost her mind. "Shyne! Let me see my nephew!"

"Sup, chica," Shyne said, embracing her foster sister before handing her baby over. The extended family shared a warm reunion right in the airport before heading over to Christi's house.

"This is..." Yolo paused to find another adjective since 'tiny' wasn't exactly a compliment.

"I know, but this is Los Angeles and houses ain't cheap," she explained as she invited her family inside the small bungalow.

"Well, I love it!" Shyne said as she took the entire tour by turning her head left and right. The open concept showed the cute kitchen, dining area and living room.

"Three bedrooms, one bath and it was only four twenty five!" Christi announced proudly.

"Four twenty five whats?" Killa asked seriously. Four hundred and twenty grand could buy a house twice this size back in Atlanta.

"Ha, ha. Very funny! Anyway, I'm delighted to have you guys come visit. My life has been so hectic trying to open my own clinic," she apologized.

"And that's why we came to you!" Yolo said and hugged her once more. "You have to show us your clinic."

"Of course. Right after we eat," Christi insisted. She showed her guest to their rooms and took them out to eat. Next they headed over to check out her clinic.

"Oh wow, this is dope!" Shyne exclaimed when they pulled up to the modest building. "My big sister is a doctor!"

"Thank you, thank you," she replied and let her family inside. Shyne memorized the codes to turn off the alarm and again when she booted up her computer.

Later that night, Yolo and Shyne came back on their own and let themselves in. Killa convinced Christi and Asad to hang out with them while they handled their business.

"Savannah Curry, age 17. Just gave birth to baby number three," Shyne said aloud as she read through Christi's files. They already had an address for Art Pence who was enjoying his last meal at a swank downtown restaurant.

"Looks like your sister did a DNA test," Yolo said, reading over her shoulder. Christi stole the father's DNA from a soda can and determined paternity.

"That's some sick shit," Shyne growled. "Not half as sick as what I'm going to do to him."

"Let your dad handle old Art and we'll take care of this deadbeat dad and beat him 'til dead," Yolo suggested. "Let's hurry up an catch up with the family."

*****

"Figures," Killa said and shook his head when he trailed Art Pence to an upscale gay club. Any man who would get rich on the pain and suffering of poor people had to take it up the ass.

He let out a deep sigh and got out of his rental car. It wasn't the only thing he rented out here in California since he secured a mountain cabin to do his dirty work. After checking his appearance he smoothed his slacks and walked in behind.

The "new meat" alarm went off amongst the regulars when the new face walked in. All eyes were on the handsome stranger with an air of mystery behind the large shades. Killa scanned the club and let his eyes adjust to the dim light. He spotted his prey at the bar and moved in.

"I'll have what he's having," Killa said as he mounted the barstool. Art put his nose up at the obvious come and waited for the come on that never came.

Killa took his drink and walked away with Art staring curiously at his back. Just like a woman the snub hit him in his femininity and he had to go investigate. He followed him to his table and stood over him.

"Can I help you?" Killa asked from behind the shades.

"You sure can," he flirted. You're not from around here, are you?"

"Nope. Just in town for the weekend. Rented a cabin in the mountains," he replied aloofly and sipped his drink. The perceived snub only made Art go harder.

"You take me up to that mountain cabin and I'm gonna eat you alive!" he said and let out a little mock growl that spread a smile on Killa's. He couldn't help but be amused at the irony.

"Bruh, if I take you up to that cabin you're the only one who's gonna get eaten alive," he shot back minus the growl for a reason.

"Let's ride then!" Art cheered and downed his drink. Killa did the same with his cola and stood.

"I'll drive," he suggested so the soon to be missing mans GPS could never link him to the cabin. Not that it mattered since they didn't make a GPS for where he was going.

"So, what do you do?" Art asked and reached for Killa's zipper. He got a Killa backhand to go along with his answer. "Feisty!"

"I'm actually retired. I turned the family business over to my kids. Sometimes I handle special cases. Mainly just for fun. You?" he answered and asked.

"I work for an insurance company. I spend my days finding creative ways to turn down claims. These sick kids can really run a check up. The more money we save the more money I get on my bonus!" he explained.

"What about the kids?" Killa asked as he reached again and got slapped again.

"Fuck them kids!" he laughed. "Shoot I got people to do and places to go!"

"Well, you're about to go somewhere tonight you've never been. Promise you that!" Killa assured him and gripped the wheel.

An hour later they arrived at the cabin at the base of the mountains. Killa led the way inside and stepped aside so Art could enter.

"Oh my!" he reeled at the strong odor in the air. "You have dogs?"

"Cats actually," he replied and pulled a pistol. Art opened his mouth to yell but Killa put a slug in his leg and gave him something to yell about.

"You think that's bad," Killa chuckled and hit a button that popped one of the bedroom doors. He backed away to the door and pulled his phone.

"What the hell is that?" Art fussed when the first of two mountain lions came out sniffing the air.

"I always get confused between puma and mountain lion," he shrugged. "Not that it really matters now."

The lions caught wind of the blood in the air and moved in. Killa scrambled to start a video call so his wife could watch.

"Oh my!" Yolo giggled when they attacked the man. One went for the open wound while the other grabbed his head. A sickening crunch echoed in the night when the lion crushed his skull. You may have to give Monte a tip."

"I'm definitely gonna have to give Monte a tip," he agreed as the lions tore him limb from limb and literally ate him alive. "Especially after y'all bring Mr. Daddy, baby-daddy up here."

"Nah, that's too easy for this dude. We gonna make him feel it!" she growled like the lady lion licking a piece of Art's spine.

"Oh my!" Killa winced. If it was worse than being eaten alive he hated for him.

*****

"I'm so sorry to have to leave you guys for a few hours, but my patients need me," Christi moaned when she prepared to leave for the clinic.

"Girl, you're a doctor! Go to work. We'll find something to do for the day," Yolo insisted.

"Hollywood!" Killa cheered and pumped his fist. Asad nodded his head in favor of the tourist trap.

"Well, we want to go to Beverly Hills," Yolo declared with Shyne by her side.

"Boys day out and girls day," Asad offered.

"Yeah, but who keeps him?" Shyne asked, pointing to their kid. She had the solution as soon as she laid out the dilemma. "Rock, paper, scissors."

"Yes!" Asad cheered when he won the first two out of three. "He's coming with us!"

"Aw man," Shyne said, twisting her lips. Generally they competed to keep their son, but Shyne deliberately threw the match so Muhammad could go with his father since she had work to do. "OK, bye-bye!"

"You gone stop biting my lines, yo," Yolo warned as they set out to kidnap Mr. Curry from his job.

"We're gonna need a change of clothes. This is going to get messy," Shyne suggested once she and her mother drove to the man's job. She loaded the tranquilizer dart into the gun so they could take him alive.

"No doubt!" Yolo laughed. They planned to get dirty by doing the man dirty. They stopped by a dollar store and bought some dollar clothes and resumed their journey.

"That's him," Shyne said when she spotted the child molester at the car lot he worked at. "Let's take him for a test drive."

"Let's," Yolo said and watched as her daughter approached the man.

"Good morning! Can I sell you a car today?" Mr. Curry asked and flashed a brilliant smile. He could get any woman he wanted with a smile like that but preferred his own daughter.

"You sure can, handsome," Shyne said flirtatiously. "Can we go for a test drive?"

"We sure can. Let's take this 2018 out for a spin," he said and pulled the keys from his pocket. He was supposed to get a copy of her ID but shrugged it off. Surely he was safe with a girl. This would be both his worst and last mistake of his life. Yolo pulled out behind them and kept her distance. She listened in on the open phone as Shyne gave him the third degree.

"So, got kids?" she inquired as she tested the steering by whipping in and out of traffic. She tested the brakes, radio and sunroof.

"Four. Two girls and two boys," he said, hoping she didn't wreck the new vehicle before she bought it.

"Got a wife or just fuck your daughter?" she asked offhandedly. Mr. Curry snapped his head in her direction.

"Who are you!" he demanded. He didn't notice her roll down the passenger side window of Yolo pull up along side.

"I'm Shyne. That's Yolo, my mom," she said, nodding towards the car next to them. Curry turned just in time to see Yolo fire a tranquilizer dart into his face. "Aw man," he groaned when he realized he was in trouble. He reached for the door handle but fell asleep before he got there. Next stop, house in the mountains.

"This guy's heavy," Shyne fussed when she and her mother half carried, half drug the man into the house.

"His daughter 'prolly says the same thing when he climbs on top of her at night," Yolo instigated to get her daughter fired up.

"Grrrr..." Shyne growled. Once they got him inside she cuffed his arms behind his back and ankles to each other. The growls and rustling of the two lions behind the door rumbled through the house.

Yolo used a pair of surgical scissors to cut his clothes off down to his drawers. She only let him keep them on because her daughter was present. Luckily for him because she would have stuffed his own dick in his mouth. What he had coming was already bad enough. It would have been that much worse with his dick in his mouth. They both changed into their Good Will clothing before Shyne stomped him awake.

"Get, yo, daughter raping, ass, up!" she demanded.

"What the... who... what?" Mr. Curry fussed, trying to figure out where he was and why. He remembered Shyne's face and test drive, but test drives never ended tied up and naked on the floor.

"Because you molested your own daughter," she explained, but that didn't explain the super sharp pairing knives in their hands.

"Her mom left me though. What was I supposed to do?" he asked as if it was justified. It wasn't and Shyne kicked a few teeth down his throat to drive that home.

"You lucky my mom's here cuz I would have stuffed your dick in your mouth before I started," Shyne growled.

"Started what? What are you going to do to me?" he pleaded.

"We're going to peel you," Yolo nodded in the same tone he used to justify his incest.

"Peel? Wha, what does that mean?" Mr. Curry wondered. "I have to get back to work."

"Peel, like a potato," Shyne said and demonstrated by removing the skin on his forehead. The man frowned before the pain registered and turned it up.

"Yeeeooow!" he screamed when Yolo joined in and peeled his arm.

"I'd save that for later," Yolo suggested since she knew what was coming next.

"What the hell is that?" Curry asked as the lions began growling and pawing at the door. The smell of blood and sound of prey worked them into a frenzy, so the mother and daughter worked even faster.

"That's about... got it," Shyne said and nodded in agreement with herself.

"He looks like he's inside out!" Yolo laughed at the now skinless man. His scream subsided to soft whimpers halfway through getting peeled.

"Time to go, Mr. Curry," Shyne said and stood. "OK, by—"

"Don't you say it!" her mother stepped in and protested. Shyne raised her bloody hands in surrender and backed away. Yolo stepped up and delivered her classic, trademarked tagline. "OK, bye-bye!"

Shyne did the honors and hit the button on their way out. The lions rushed out and got on his ass. Mr. Curry didn't even put up a fuss as they tore him apart and ate him alive. The ladies changed back into their clothes and headed back to the city. Christi would now be able to contact family to save the girl from her prison.

Chapter Sixteen

'Dear 1-800-Killa. My name is Fletcher Wilcox. I own a computer firm here in Birmingham. Alabama, not England. My life and marriage were just ruined by allegations of sexual misconduct. I never, ever even thought about stepping outside of my marriage. This money hungry whore I hired lied on me. This climate of "me too"' prejudiced a female judge to rule against me. I lost my business, marriage and money while this tramp lives it up on my dime. Kill her, please...'

"OK," Shyne said with a simple shrug. It's a new day where women are standing up for themselves against powerful men who used their power to prey on women. Bravo for them, no more suffering in silence. Forced to share space at work or family functions with the same sick fuck that touched them without permission. Unfortunately, some con-women took advantage of the anguish for personal gain.

Terry Clark was one such woman. She had more cleavage than skills when she showed up for a job interview. Her bra held more than her brain and resume, so she made sure to show off with a low cut blouse. Fletcher felt sorry for her and wanted to give her a chance. She mistook his act of charity as interest and threw her well used vagina at him on a regular basis. He threatened to fire her over her frequent advances and she turned the tables on him by saying, "Me, too".

She sued him and took half of his business. His wife filed for divorce and took the other half. Terry grew up sucking clits and dicks in trailer parks and trucks stops and had no problem seducing the lonely divorcee. Fletcher lived alone in a one-bedroom apartment while they bumped coochies in the house he built from the ground up.

"Babe, I have a job over in Alabama. Wanna come?" Shyne asked her husband even though she knew the answer.

"Nah," he declined as expected. Asad was a homebody and preferred to be in his own home when not at work.

"I know, baby. I'm sorry. I won't be long. I can drive over, 'fix it' and come right back," she pouted. She paused and waited for him to say 'no' and she wouldn't go. He didn't, so she packed one of her bags for the trip.

"The baby is sleep so..." Asad said and motioned towards the bed.

"So, let's get it," she cheered in a whisper so they didn't wake him up. They slipped into the bed and into each until both were spent. A mutual shower followed and Shyne set off to handle her business.

Her first stop was the small house her parents bought to store their weapons. They slowly brought some items from the New York house as well as new items they accumulated along the way. Shyne packed a second bag with tools from her trade.

"Oooh, Terry! I'm gonna do you real bad!" she said, shaking her head as she selected a new device. The Shyne-inator 2000 delivered 3rd degree bones, but this new contraption bumped it up a notch.

*****

'Breaking news, breaking news! A white child has gone missing in North Carolina! All hands on deck. A white child is missing!' the news reporter reported urgently.

"Look at this shit!" Yolo fussed and twisted her lips at the news report. Black children were going missing at an alarming rate, but barely got a mention in local news, let alone national news.

"Gonna have your daughter beat her up, too?" Killa cracked up. He got a serious kick out of Shyne beating up the Louisville reporter. It took months for her to heel up enough to go back to work. Even with makeup she still didn't look the same.

"Nah I—" she began to say, but was cut off when the missing girl's mother and boyfriend popped on the screen. The stringy haired trailer trash stole her whole attention. She knew in an instant they had something to do with the girl's disappearance.

"Darla was in her bed and somebody took-ed her. She woke-ed up 'round midnight and Darryl sent-ed her back to bed," the woman drawled in a low county twang. Her boyfriend, Darryl, nodded and darted his beady eyes.

"Bullshit," Killa decided and reached for his phone. It was late, but Sun answered it quickly. "Pack a bag. You're going to North Carolina."

"I just saw that. I'm already on it," he replied loud enough to wake his sleeping wife. She stirred, blinked awake and sat up to make sure he was OK.

"Find out what they did to that child and do the same to them," Killa ordered.

"Worse! Do them worse!" Yolo called out from his side. An eye for an eye is great, but overkill is always in order when kids are concerned.

"Your mom said..."

"Worse. Yeah, I heard it. I'm on it. Talk to you later, God willing," he said and clicked off. "Did I wake you?"

"Yes, but what's wrong?" Bryonna asked. She loved her husband and was ready to fix whatever was wrong.

"My bad," he said as if he didn't mean to wake her, even though he did. "Just gotta go to North Carolina to handle some business for my mom and dad."

"Oh," she said even though she still had no idea what Killa and Yolo actually did. She was now a doctor herself, but Sun's barbershops paid for their comfortable life. The couple had plans to go house shopping soon.

"But... since you're up..." he offered. She smiled wickedly, nodded and accepted.

*****

"Turn down for what?" Terry wanted to know as she popped another bottle of champagne. She had been turning straight up since she came up off her latest scam.

"Turn down for nothing!" her new girlfriend shot back. She leaned back and spread her legs for the champagne fountain. Terry poured the expensive grapes on her new breast, down her tucked tummy and between her legs. Terry was right there to slurp up the mixture of champagne and vagina juice.

Terry sucked a nut out of her and switched places so she could get sucked off, too. She kicked her legs open to expose her reconstructed vagina and her girlfriend dug in. She was new to eating coochie, but how hard can it be? It's pretty much self-explanatory and soon Terry was kicking, clawing and coming. It was a good one, but she didn't get to bask in it.

"Y'all just nasty," Shyne grimaced as she came out of the darkness. Terry scrambled to hit the light and they all got a shock.

"Who are you!" Terry demanded and she stood and balled her fist. She had a mean fight game from growing up in trailer parks. Trailer parks are white people projects and just as rough. It was a good question, but Shyne had one of her own.

"You?" she shrieked when she realized who the girlfriend was. "What are you doing here? With her?"

"I go where the money goes," Fletcher's ex wife said with a shrug. "I know his punk behind didn't send you?"

"I know!" Terry laughed and high fived. "I don't know who sent you, but I'm 'fixin to send you back with a whooped ass."

"A fist fight? Cool!" Shyne cheered and sat her weapons behind her. If Terry got past her she would be in trouble. "Let's get it!"

"Let's," Terry snarled and moved in. She threw a sweet combination of punches, but Shyne dipped, ducked and swayed out of the way.

She fired off a combo of her own and connected with each punch. She left a knot and lump everywhere her blows landed.

"Kick her ass!" the ex Mrs. Fletcher urged. Terry knew already she couldn't whoop her, but didn't want to punk out in front of her girlfriend.

"Ugh!" she grunted and gunged for the weapons behind Shyne. Shyne grabbed her arm and twisted it until it popped and dangled uselessly by her side.

"What do you want?" Terry pleaded. She was ready to give whatever it was so she could leave.

"Justice," Shyne said and aimed the new device. She aimed at her face and fired a stream of fluid that erased her skin and flesh down to the bone. Even Shyne was shocked at the results. "Whoa!"

"Yeeow!" she howled as the hydrochloric acid chewed her up. The girlfriend seen all she needed to see and took off for the door. She made a run for it but people need feet to run.

"Nuh uh," Shyne giggled and shot a stream of acid at her feet, turning them into skeleton feet. She turned back to the whimpering Terry and gave her a blast to her chest. It ate her flesh and bones and exposed her beating heart. It took a few more beats and stopped. She then turned back to the hollering woman and sprayed her head. The acid ate up her hair, scalp and skull until her brain fell out the hole. "That'll shut up your holler. I'll holler! That's it! I found my tagline!"

Shyne hacked into the women's computers and phones and found information implicated the women in the rouse. A few clicks transferred what was left of the money back to Fletcher. He lost a great deal, but some is better than none. She stumbled across a tidbit of new information and added another stop to her visit.

*****

Judge Judith Simons was a bull daggin', man hating, penis envy having poor excuse for a judge. She had no business presiding over the case since she took money from Terry. They left a paper trail that led danger to her doorstep.

"Who?" Judith asked and headed towards the door. She assumed it was the carpet she ordered to munch on from the escort service.

"Meeee," Shyne called out like people do on a Facebook post giving away free books.

"Oooh, choco-latte!" the dyke cheered and licked her thin lips. She stepped aside so Shyne could enter. Just like a dude, she copped a feel on her booty when she passed by. Shyne whirled and slapped a spark out of her just like she did dudes. "Oooh, mama likes it rough!"

"Well, I'm here to give it to you rough," Shyne assured her as she looked around the nicely appointed home. "You here alone?"

"I'm home alone," she said and nodded. She smiled her last smile to match the one on her guest's face. "And I'm gonna eat you alive!"

"Actually, I'm going to beat you to death," Shyne nodded with her and attacked. The old lady didn't know what hit her when Shyne began to hit her. It reminded her of beating a punching bag in the gym. Except a punching bag doesn't give out satisfying grunts and moans when you beat it. Judge Judith was already knocking on death's door when Shyne took her head in her arms. She gave it a quick twist like a chicken and hit her with a "I'll holler!"

Chapter Seventeen

"Wait... you said what?" Yolo asked, stopping Shyne's story.

"I said, 'I'll holler'. It's my tagline since you tripping about your funky little saying. Now, I got my own. I'll holler."

"Yeah, but still. That's so whack!" she howled. Shyne twisted her lips as her mother got a good laugh at her expense.

"Any... way. Yo, did you see the news? They stole like three black babies from the hospital! Fresh out the oven and gone," Shyne said, shaking her head. She looked over at her toddler, toddling around the den and sighed. "The anguish..."

"What the heck is going on? Black kids going missing all over the country," Yolo fussed. "Your father and I are gonna get to the bottom of this. And when we do—"

"Me and my twin gonna make them wish they was never born," Shyne growled.

"Speaking of goofy, where is he?"

"He went up to Nawf Cackalaki to see about the little missing girl."

"The little white girl all over the news? Oh, her tweeker mama and her mama boyfriend did something to that child!" Shyne fussed. She was still fussing when her bff Bryonna walked in.

"Guess what!" Bryonna cheered and braced herself to deliver the news.

"You're pregnant!" Yolo and Shyne called out at the same time.

"How you guys know? I just took the test," she wondered with a curious frown.

"Um, you're a newlywed. I'm surprised it took this long," Yolo added as a matter of fact.

"Yeah, I was wondering if my brother was shooting blanks," Shyne added causally. She and her mother went back and forth about him like she wasn't there.

"Um, hello?" Bryonna called, waving a hand to be seen. "That's my husband, you know?"

"Yeah, poor thing. Married to the slob. I mean, mob," Yolo laughed. It was all in fun because she adored her first born. She was proud of the man he had become and knew he was going to do her proud up in North Carolina.

*****

Sun crept by the missing girls trailer and spotted FBI surveillance vans. They knew the mother's boyfriend had everything to do with it, so they waited and watched for him to fuck up. He weighed his options and decided he'd come around from the woods and kidnap the couple. That was easier said than done for a city boy like Sun.

"Shit, fuck, got danggit!" Sun grumbled and griped as he was assaulted by all kinds of bugs and insects. They buzzed in his ears and eyes until one flew into his mouth. He was at a loss as to how to get it out so he did what he always did when he got in trouble.

"Hey, baby. You're done already?" Yolo asked when she took her beloved son's call. "You are your mother's son!"

"No, mom. I'm in the woods and a ga-nat flew in my eye," he whispered so he wouldn't blow his cover.

"A what?" she asked and sat up. Killa sat up too to make sure everything was okay.

"A ga-nat. It's in my eye!" he fussed. "They're everywhere! I'm under attack."

"What's a ga-nat?" Yolo asked, getting concerned now. She was ready to roll out and declare war on all ga-nats if they were attacking her first born. Killa just cracked up laughing and laid back down.

"A ga-nat. Gnat, ga-nat!" he explained. There was a brief silence as his mother processed the new information.

"Your son on the phone," she said and tossed the phone to her husband.

"Bruh, just use your eyelashes to get it out," he explained and explained how to do it. He waited on the line until he was OK.

"Thanks, pops. I got it. Let me talk back to mom," he said.

"She's...." Killa said, looking down at his wife with her mouth full of him.

"Eating."

"Oh OK. Well, I'm here. I'm about to find out where that baby is," Sun growled.

"What you guys doing?

"Oh, the usual," he said and clicked off. Sun twisted his lips at the abrupt end of the conversation. He shrugged his shoulders and pressed on.

The FBI was parked out front so he slipped into the back of the trailer. He checked his silencer equipped gun and eased inside.

"My turn on the slave, Darrrrl," the child's mother moaned as Darryl took a long pull on their shared meth chalis.

"He's a hog," his brother complained. He and his girlfriend also stayed in the trailer. Darryl ignored their pleas and kept on toking. His eyes went wide from the inhalation of the deadly drug, but they went even wider when he saw the black man with a gun enter the room.

"Who are you!" Darryl's brother demanded and stood. Sun threw a hard right hook that broke both his jaw and neck at the same time. He crumpled down dead as a doorknob on the spot.

"Anyone else have any questions?" Sun wanted to know. All heads shook 'no' since no one wanted the same answer he gave the dead guy. "Good. Now, I have a question of my own. Where's the girl?"

"I don't know!" the mother spoke up. Sun shrugged and shot the other woman in her face. The trailer wall was decorated in a nasty pink mixture of blood, bone and brain matter. The mother took a look at it and pointed at Darryl. "He took her somewhere!"

"Where? Where is she Darryl? You tell the truth and I won't shoot you," Sun vowed.

"I tried to sell her, but no one wants little white girls. They all want LNB's," he explained.

"What's an LNB?" Sun asked looking between the two survivors.

"Little Nigga Babies. It's the new craze," the mother explained. "W.L.M sells them for good money, so we thought we could sell Brittany. She would go to a better home and we could buy more drugs."

"But no one wanted her so..." Darryl said and shrugged. Sun felt his blood begin to boil as he translated the shrug.

"So, what?" he asked through clenched teeth.

"I just buried her. Didn't have the heart to kill her so I just put her in the ground and, buried her."

Sun crossed the room in a blur and rammed the gun so far down his throat half his hand was in his mouth. He tugged on the trigger blasting his skull away until his hand came out the back of his head.

"Want some head? White girl head?" the mother asked, hoping to save herself.

"Only if you tell me where she was buried?" he bargained. He aimed her own phone at her as she confessed and gave directions to her child's grave. He posted it to her own social media account as he slipped the DC 2000 over her head. He hit the switch and got him some white girl head.

Sun took the severed head with him and found the gravesite. He sat her mother's head on top and left. He left with more questions than answers but it was time to go home.

*****

"Mmm, great to be home!" Sun sighed in satisfaction to his wife's welcome home.

"Great to have you home, big daddy," Bryonna replied and snuggled up next to him. That was her 15th time calling him daddy since he arrived but Sun wasn't good with hints. "Anyway, guess what?"

"You're pregnant?" he actually guessed.

"Who told you? Shyne? Your mom? That's messed up!" she popped up and fussed.

"No one told me! You said guess what, so I guessed. Wait, you are?" he exclaimed and sat straight up in bed.

"I am. You're going to be a father!" she said happily. The couple hugged and kissed until they ended up back where they started. They drifted off to sleep so they could go visit his parents the next day. After getting a shower and getting dressed, they headed out to the suburbs.

"We should buy something out here," Sun saaid as they neared his parents' house. Killa and Yolo bought several acres so they could have some privacy.

"It's pricey out here?" Bryonna questioned. She knew his barber-shops did well, but one needed to be doing great to live out here. She often wondered what Mr. and Mrs. Forrest did, but never got an answer. Always some wild stories about being hitmen and women.

"Mmhm," he said, meaning she wasn't getting an answer today either. He was happy that Shyne was present when he arrived so she could keep her company while he briefed his parents. Shyne had other ideas though.

"Hey, little mama!" Shyne cheered and steered her friend away. She pawned her son off on her and rushed to join the family meeting.

"Saw the news?" Yolo chuckled fondly as she hugged her son. She appreciated the way he led police to the child's body and used the mother's head as a landmark.

"I did. At least that baby can get a proper burial," Sun said with his emotions written on his face.

"Speaking of babies, congratulations, son," Killa said and gave him a pound.

"Thanks, pop," he said and stuck his chest out. It was a warm father-son moment until Shyne fucked it up.

"If it's a boy you can name him La-Loyd," she said and cracked her parents up. They knew his strange language would turn the name Lloyd into La-Loyd.

"Anyway, what the heck is the WLM? Dude said they're selling black kids. LNB's they call it," he asked.

"Grrrr," Shyne growled at the search results. "Little Nigga Babies. Look it!"

"Grrrr," Yolo seconded when she saw the latest craze. Rich white girls and women holding little black children like lap dogs. "Every since Kim had a half black child everyone wants one!"

"WLM? The bar in South Carolina," Killa recalled. His killer smile spread on his and Yolo's faces at the fond memory of the red neck bar.

"Dude down in New Orleans, too!" Sun recalled. "I seen it on some of his papers,"

"White lives matter. It's a white supremacy group. They're the ones holding the retreat in a few months!" Yolo reminded.

"Yeah and the Killa clan is going to crash the party!" Killa snarled as his mind twisted and twirled. "This is gonna be a family affair. I'm calling Rico and Xavier down for this one. Even grandma gonna want in on this."

"Well, if it's a family affair then maybe you should call your cousin," Yolo suggested. "And his daughter, too."

"The Dope Boy and Dope Girl down with the Killa clan? Oh, that's going to be epic! Pass me my phone..."

Chapter eighteen

"Giddy up, lil mama," he said while she rode him low and slow like a good cowgirl should. Backwards, with a shimmy on the top stroke, then a wiggle and squeeze when she bottomed out. Do, try this at home.

"Ooh wee," she moaned when she neared her destination. She was driving, so she took the quickest route to orgasm-ville.

"Ooh wee is right!" he said when her vagina dispensed a good creamy coating on his shaft. She was on the verge of busting a nut, but he was right behind her. He was so glad he was aiming his phone at it and getting it all on tape. The sights and sounds were captured in brilliant high definition to marvel at later. Reverse cowgirl allow men to star in their own porno film. A win/win if ever there was one. It was so right until it went so wrong.

"Shit!" she fussed when his phone began to ring. Not just any phone, but the special satellite phone that stayed charged and always got answered. She may have fussed, but she reached over and grabbed it off the nightstand and passed it behind her. Luckily for both, he had enough wood to stay inside. She kept right on rocking on that wood, too. Rock, wiggle, shimmy, squeeze.

"Yo, mmm. What's good, Killa," Cameron drawled in his east side twang and kept filming and moaning. The cousins lived on opposite suburban sides of the same city, but rarely hung out. They were best friends, but both were on their grown man shit. Grown men stay home with wives and children. Cam would pick up their grandmother for church twice a month without fail. His calling on this phone meant it was business, not personal.

"You need to call me back?" Killa asked, hearing moans on Cam's end of the phone.

"Yeah, but it won't be but a minute," he said and clicked off the line. Michelle grabbed his ankles and slung her ass wildly and got her rocks off. Her vaginal walls contracted and convulsed, causing him to join her. Good thing her tubes were tied tightly because he almost untied them when he exploded. "Yee Haa!"

"Yee Haa is right daddy," she said as she dismounted and turned around to cuddle up. As expected, he picked the phone back up called his cousin back.

"Sup yo, what's popping? Mmhm. Un huh. Say what? Hells yeah!" he said as Killa filled him on the missing kids and the White Lives Matter movement. He was on board to join the mission to destroy the movement until Killa mentioned his adopted daughter. His biological children all lived in the city, but none were 'bout that life' like she was. "I'on know, cuz. She's a loose cannon."

"This a war, yo. We need cannons. Even loose ones," he reminded him. Cam twisted his lips thoughtfully and knew he was right.

"Yeah, you right. I'll give her a call. We'll bring her up when the time comes and turn her loose," he agreed. He watched his wife kiss her way down his torso in search of attention. She got his full attention when her hot mouth engulfed him. "Welp, gotta go,"

"Me t—" Killa started to say before he hung up.

There was no need to call back since Yolo was kissing her way down his torso, as well. It was one of those rainy Saturday afternoon where there's nothing much better to do except fuck. They set their younger children up with lunch and movies and went upstairs to be lunch and make movies.

"Don't forget to call your daughter," Michelle said once she and Cam wrapped up round two. She knew from experience he'd be sleeping in a few minutes.

"Yeah," he agreed and reached for the satellite phone once more. He could have used her cell, but knew this one would get answered no matter what she was doing.

"Yeeeee Haaaaaa!" Camiesha howled and rode hard like a young cowgirl should. Her wet vagina squished and squelched so loudly, Trigga leaned up to watch. Quite the feat since he was blind.

"I can almost see it!" he said, holding on to her round ass cheeks as she bounced backwards on his dick.

"Well, watch this!" she said and came all over his dick. He couldn't see the gush of juice that exploded from her juice box, but felt it all it ran down his balls and puddled underneath them.

"Shit!" he shouted and went over the edge himself. It was a good one, but got cut short by the satellite phone.

"Uh oh," she moaned, hoping it wasn't bad news. Her beloved great grandmother got older by the day and knew one day this phone would be the bearer of bad news. She braced herself and took the call.

"Hey, daddy."

"Are you OK? You sound strange?" Cam asked, hearing remnants of her busting a nut a minute earlier.

"I'm great. How's grandma?" she wanted to know.

"She's good. I am, too. Can you talk?" he asked. He had just stepped in the shower so he could talk freely. His wife knew he was an ex goon, but he still kept certain things from her.

"One sec," she said and rolled out of bed. Trigga watched her round ass shift from sound and memory as she stepped out onto the private balcony off the bedroom. He too knew not to ask questions where her family was concerned. "OK, what's up, pops?"

"You ever hear of White Lives Matter? It's a white supremacy group. They're behind the rash of missing black kids lately. They sell them as pets and slaves," he explained.

"Is that why I see these white girls with little black kids all over my timeline?" CAmiesha moaned.

"Girl, I know your 'wanted in a death penalty case ass' isn't on social media?" Cam fussed.

"Um, no," she said, scrambling to deactivate her page, knowing he was currently searching. He typed in 'Dope Girl' and just missed it before she shut it down. "But anyway, you know I'm down. Count me in."

"OK, baby, but strictly business when you come. No clubbing, no turning up!" he warned sternly.

"OK, daddy!" she replied like she was really gonna listen. Anyone who knows Camiesha Forrest knows good and well she was going clubbing and turning up when she got back to Atlanta.

*****

"Yeee Haaa!" Shyne shouted and shook in satisfaction since it was rainy downtown Atlanta, too. She dismounted her husband and spun around to cuddle. She didn't get to cuddle long before her husband began to snore. Poor fellow didn't get much rest since it was raining all week. She patted herself on the back and rolled out of bed. She was getting board, so she checked out what the hot line had to offer.

Dear 1-800- Killa, can you please kill someone for me? Not just anybody, my ex, if I can call him that. His name is Maurice and he gave me HIV. He knew he had it. He knew I am a single mom and he still didn't spare me. Then when I get to the clinic, I find out he gave it to a lot of girls. They say I can live a long life if I eat healthy and take my meds, but what about getting married one day? What about having more kids one day? He destroyed my life. Please kill him.'

"My pleasure!" Shyne said. She scoured the Killa site for local losers so she wouldn't have to travel. She followed the social media links the victim gave and found Maurice's smiling face. He was a pretty boy, with a pretty smile that made it easier for him to attract the young women he preyed upon.

"Um, how about Kenyatta, Jackson," she guessed as she set up her new fake profiles. She, like most chicks, had plenty of them for various reasons, but this one was just for him. A spider web set to catch a cockroach. She posted a stolen pic and the trap was set. He accepted her friend request, 'liked' her pic and in-boxed 'hello sexy' in under a minute. "Whoa!"

"Hello, yourself,'" she said along as she typed her reply. He shot a quick dick pic in reply. Shyne giggled and blushed as she deleted it. She shot a glance over to her sleeping husband who had the only dick she wanted in her inbox or in her box.

'Your turn,' he typed back. Shyne googled vagina and picked one out for him. 'Nice! I wanna taste it,' he shot back immediately.

"Bet you do with yo' nasty ass," she fussed and put his picture in her family's specialized program. It compared the photo to national databases and spit an answer back in minutes. "Ralph Henderson. Age 30."

Ralph had been convicted in Florida for the same offense of knowingly spreading the virus that causes AIDS. He served a few years there and moved here to start all over again. She compared the address he gave via inbox to the one returned by their program and decided to pay him a visit.

*****

"Got a date?" Paula fussed as her live in boyfriend got dressed to impress. She knew he cheated on her on a regular basis, but was too happy to have the pretty boy living with her to kick him out. She lost a little self-esteem with every pound she gained. She now tipped the scales at 350 with zero self-esteem.

"Date? Nah, more like a meeting," Ralph said with a chuckle. He didn't mind using women to get what he needed or where he needed to be. "I just broke you off, so stop complaining."

"You did, too," she said, giggling as she covered her mouth. He didn't pay bills or help out around the house, but he was laying plenty of pipe. She could pay the bills on her own, but couldn't lay any pipe. "Need a ride? Some money?"

"Yeah I—" he said when the doorbell interrupted their conversation. He looked curiously at her, but she shrugged since she wasn't expecting company. He went over and peeped through the peephole. He saw the pretty girl and snatched it open. "Hello, you looking for Beatrice or Maurice?"

"Nope," Shyne said, pushing inside. "I'm looking for you, Ralph."

"Who?" both occupants asked in confusion. She knew him as Maurice and he wondered who she was who knew who he was. Nothing good was ever associated with his real name. His fist instinctively balled up ready for danger. He had no idea just how much danger he was in.

"You may as well put those up," she giggled at him, bringing fist to a gunfight and produced a gun.

"What's going on here, Maurice? Who is this girl? I know you don't be having girls in my house!" Beatrice fussed and balled her meaty fist.

"You got bigger problems that that, sis," Shyne advised and passed her his paperwork. Ralph knew what was in it and made a move. Not a very good move since Shyne put a silent slug in his ankle. He let out a blood-curdling scream. It was loud, but nothing compared to Beatrice.

"H...I...V! Boy, do you have HIV? Did you give me HIV!" she shouted inches from his face.

"Sure did. Gave a bunch of women HIV," Shyne instigated. It didn't take much instigating for the woman to attack. She pummeled and pounded him with her chubby fist. When her hands began to hurt she stood up and stomped him. Shyne just aimed her phone to get it all on video. It wouldn't cure the dangerous virus, but at least his victims get the satisfaction of watching him get beaten to death.

"Did you kill me? Huh! Huh!" she demanded as the playboy broke and buckled under her feet.

"Uh sis, I don't think he can hear you," Shyne said since she knew a dead body when she saw one. She came to do it herself, but this was better. Same outcome, but much more fun to watch.

"Oh no! I killed him! I'm going to jail," she wailed and broke down.

"Only if you want to," Shyne offered. "Or you can go see a movie and I'll take care of this."

"Who are you?" Beatrice asked and cocked her head curiously.

"If I told you, I'd have to kill you. Or you can go see a movie and I'll take care of this?"

"So, is Bad Cop still playing?" she asked, deciding to leave.

"It is and it's dope!" Shyne said. The woman cleaned herself up to go while Shyne called her brother to bring their cleaning supplies. Saws and bags to break him down into disposable pieces. "One more thing, sis. Go get checked out."

"Thank you," Beatrice said with a sigh and a nod before turning to leave. When she returned hours later, there was no trace that a murder just occurred.

Chapter nineteen

'Dear 1-800-Killa, my grandbaby Ricky just got convicted of armed robbery and got a life sentence. He did it and he should go to jail, but his friend snitched on him and got probation. It was all Cheiva's idea and he's at home while my Ricky gone to prison. To make matters worse, Chieva lied on my baby and said he told on him. He got killed as soon as he touched the yard. I know you can't bring him back, but you can send Chieva's bitch ass with him? Kill him, make it ugly.'

"Ugly, coming right up! You want in on this?" Sun asked as he and Shyne went over the local complaints. Decatur Georgia was an east side suburb with plenty of bad people in need of dead, and they were about to get it.

"Hells yeah! The only question is how ugly?" she snarled. Snitches get stitches in general, but this one called for extremes.

"Super ugly!" he said and furrowed his brow in thought. She did the same and they brainstormed on the best way to give him the worst possible death.

"Well, me and mom peeled that guy out in LA?" Shyne offered as a solution. "She sure made it sound like it hurt. It was definitely ugly! He looked like he was turned inside out!"

"Eh," he said, shrugging. It did sound good, so he didn't discount it. He loved the mountain lion move, but was hating because he didn't get in on it. "Something like that."

Shyne smiled at her twin brother as the wheels turned in his head. She knew he was trying to put a spin on her idea to make it his own. She didn't mind since she knew it spawned from her, and it didn't really matter as long as his skin came off. This was one snitch who wouldn't have nothing left to stitch. Maybe she could have a snitch skin purse made. Or snitch shoes, belt, whatever as long as it was ugly.

"Ooh and look!" Shyne fussed and pointed at Chieva's social media page. He was pouring out a little liquor and blowing smoke in the air for his dead homie.

'*Yo, dis 'fo my boi, Ricky. That's fucked up what happened to you, shawty. Don't worry, I'ma make dem niggas feel it 'fo what dey did to you, shawty.*'

"So, pairing knives, huh?" Sun nodded. Peeling him suddenly sounded good.

"Yeah, but where we gonna get a mountain lion, though?" she asked, twisting her lips in thought. "We could ask dad?"

"Nah, we got this. I'll come up with something," he quickly shot down. Sun was coming into his own and that meant not running back to his father every time he had a problem. No, he was calling his mommy.

"You two didn't have enough time together in the womb?" Bryonna complained when she found Sun and Shyne huddled over a computer screen. She loved how close the Forrest family was and was delighted to be a part of it. "You're supposed to be on the grill aren't you, mister?"

"She won't leave me alone," Sun said and lead his wife away. He and Shyne would meet up the next day to attend Ricky's funeral service.

*****

Sun and Shyne met up the next day for Ricky's funeral. Seeing and hearing his broken hearted mother wail and break down only made it that much worse on Chieva. It went from worse to worst when Chieva came into the church to show his respect. Impossible since he didn't have any respect for himself or anyone else. He went to the open casket and gasped at what lay inside.

"Damn, shawty!" he exclaimed and staggered back when he saw his one time friend. The results of getting beaten to death were more than he expected. His mother took a page out of history and displayed him like Emmett Till.

"Damn nothing, you bitch ass, snitch ass, fuck ass—" Ricky's mom berated as she charged him. "You did this!"

"I ain't did shit! It was all his idea!" Chieva lied as he backed away. The ushers held the grieving mother back while he backed all the way out of the church.

"Let's go," Shyne advised needlessly since her brother already began to stand. They rushed out behind him and kept an eye on him as they went to their rental car. Chieva got in his bucket and pulled off with Sun and Shyne on his tail.

Shyne would lure him to the abandoned house they secured for the day. It was good it was due to be completely renovated because it was about to become a crime scene. They waited until he stopped for burgers and Shyne hopped out to make her move.

"Meet me at the spot. We'll be there in a few," she advised over her shoulder. Sun shrugged because he still didn't get what dudes saw in his sister but it always worked like a charm.

"A'ight, yo," he said and pulled off. He still hadn't secured a mountain lion, but did get the next best thing. The mother wanted ugly and she was going to get it.

"Sup sexy?" Chieva asked and cocked his head to the side with a crooked smile. He ran his eyes up and down Shyne's curves and came back up to her pretty face.

"Sup with you?" she shot back seductively and licked her lips. When his smile widened, it was all the equivalent of a fisherman feeling a nibble. All that was left was to snatch him out of the water.

"Just came from my boi Ricky funeral. Tyna eat, drank, smoke and fuck something. You feel me?" he asked and struck a pose.

"I'm about to feel you."

"Let's get up out of here," he suggested and extended hand.

"Hole up, lemme grab something for my brother. He loves this spot!" she said truthfully. Chieva shrugged it off when she paid for her own food. Moments later, they hopped in his car and followed her directions the house of future horror.

"You stay here?" he asked skeptically as he pulled up the the vacant house.

"Yup," she said and hopped out before he could question her any further. She put some sway in her hips knowing he would follow and he did. Shyne pretended to use a key and opened the door when he caught up on the front porch.

"Dang shawty, we can go to my house. I—" he was saying until Shyne spun and hit him with a tranquilizer in his throat. He knew he was in trouble when the room began to dim and spin. "Uh oh."

"Uh oh is right," Shyne chuckled and got down to work. She cuffed his wrists behind his back and ankles to each other. Sun arrived and walked straight inside with a bag of tricks.

"I don't know how you do it," he said, shaking his head at the subdued man sleeping on the floor. She shrugged and they began removing tools of their trade from the bag. Coveralls covered their clothes to prevent them from being covered in blood. Foam earplugs would dim the inevitable screams when they got to work.

"Did you get a mountain lion?" Shyne asked and felt silly for asking. This was the same guy who had to video call from the store to be able to get the right thing. One time his wife asked for pads and got pull-ups instead.

"Of course not!" he laughed. "Fuck I'ma get a mountain lion from? I got something else that might work. Worked for mom."

Shyne smiled brightly as she guessed what he brought. It was a page she shared from their mother's diary being resurrected through the kids. She sometimes shared tidbits from the diary, but most of it was a secret mother and daughter shared.

"Well, let's wake this snitch up," she said and pulled the pairing knives and pliers from the bag. She passed one each to her brother and they got down to work. Sun used surgical scissors to remove his clothes before they removed his skin.

"Hmph?" Chieva asked curiously when a sharp pain snapped him from his deep sleep. He frowned when he saw Shyne pulling his skin from his legs. "Yeeow!"

"Yeow is right," Sun said as he used the knife and pliers on the back of his neck. He got it started and began to pull his scalp over his head and face.

"You giving him an autopsy before he dead!" Shyne giggled then grimaced when he accomplished his task. "Ooh ooh! Remember that movie, *Face Off*?"

"This the remix!" Sun said. He had to say it loud to be heard over his screams and moans. They laughed and joked as they skinned him alive. Once they finished, it was time for him to die.

"Well, that's pretty ugly," Shyne nodded and took a picture for the grieving mother.

"And it's about to get even uglier," he said and rushed outside. Sun returned a few minutes later with two large dogs on leashes. They pulled him towards the smell of blood. The dogs were ready to tear the man up, but Shyne ran over and hugged the huge dogs.

"Presa de Carnirio! My favorites," she squealed and hugged the confused pooches. The boy dog turned and looked at Sun like, 'TF?'

"Yeah, but," he said and pointed at the whimpering man. The poor fellow had screamed himself horse from being skinned and could only moan and groan.

"My bad," she said, raising her hands in surrender. She stepped aside and watched as the dogs attacked.

"Just like a chick," Sun laughed as the girl dog rushed between his legs and snatched his genitals away. That got another good scream out of him as Shyne recorded it for Ricky's mom. The boy dog clamped down on his throat and crushed his windpipe. The man was skinned alive, then eaten to death and that's super ugly.

Chapter twenty

'Dear 1-800-Killa, I, feel silly but I need to vent, so... OK, so my name is Tisha. I work with children services in Miami. We just removed a child from a home because she was going to school hungry and dirty. So, I just spoke with the girl and she told me the craziest story. So crazy I don't know what to think.'

"Get yo' little ass in here, Bertha!" Mrs, McCoy *fussed at her new foster child. She couldn't afford to buy a little black child like rich folk, so the foster child service was the next best thing. Not only would they give her a free kid, but cut a check every month to boot.*

"But my name is Jamesha," *the pretty little girl reminded her once more.*

"Gal, she said yo' name is Bertha and that's what it is!" *Mr. McCoy demanded.* "Now, if you wanna eat, you gonna work!"

Crazy right? But she was serious. They wouldn't feed her. Threatened to whip her or sell her and.

"And they about to get fucked up!" Yolo growled hotly. Child abuse was one thing they couldn't stomach or stand. Little Jamesha was safe and sound, but the McCoys were in trouble. They weren't the only ones though.

"Aww, man," Killa lamented when the video of a child in Orlando played on the news. The special needs boy gave a heart wrenching appeal to stop the bullies from bullying him. The video had got national attention and went viral. A local college football team made a show by coming to the school to eat lunch with him. The bullying stopped for a whole day and resumed the next.

"Alexis, call the den," Killa told the device on the night stand.

"I really wish you would get rid of that thing. It ordered fifteen bibles last week!" Yolo fussed.

"That's because you was screaming 'oh God,'" he reminded her and cracked up.

"Yes, father?" little Diedra said so sweetly and calmly through the new aged intercom, her mother sucked her teeth.

"They up to something," Yolo said surely. She was only sure because she knew her kids.

"Of course they are," he agreed and called them upstairs. "You and your brother come up to our room.

"Your room? Y'all got clothes on?" the fussy little girl fussed into the intercom.

"Girl, get yo' little ass up here!" Yolo demanded and turned it off. "Gone ask us if we got clothes on! Who does she think she is?"

"I'on know, but let's put some clothes on before they come up here," Killa suggested and rolled out of bed. He slipped on some sweats while she rolled into a robe. A moment later, little Killa pushed open their door.

"Little boy, what did I tell you about knocking on our door?" Yolo snapped at her son.

"That I'm 'posed to," he said, making a face like it was a silly question. He knew the rule, but never followed it.

"Yeah, you need to knock cuz you don't want to see what I saw!" Diedra said, flipping her hair and rolling her eyes. "Y'all just nasty."

"Your mama nasty," Killa laughed until a glance from his wife wiped his smile away. "Um, so anyway. Look at this."

Yolo stifled a smile at the frowns and scowls that spread on her babies' faces. They were just happily playing video games in the den. Now they were 38 hot, watching the distraught kid.

"How does that make you feel?" Yolo asked her daughter once the bullying video ended.

"Grrrr," she replied and clenched her little fist.

"Makes me wanna beat them up," little Killa added and balled his fists up, as well.

"Well, we're going to Disney this weekend. Maybe you will see them," Killa casually tossed out. That brought smiles to their little faces.

They high-fived each other at either going to Disney or the chance to meet and beat the bullies. They turned to leave, but not before Diedra twisted her lips up at her mother.

"Nasty," she huffed and lifted her head to march out of their bedroom.

"I got your nasty, little girl!" Yolo said and made a move to go after her.

"Chill, baby," Killa said as he held her back. "Remember, she did walk in on you doing your backwards cowgirl thing."

"Yeee Ha!" she giggled and blushed. "Anyway, I know what you're doing. Them bullies are 11 and 12. Diedra and Killa are 5 and 7. That's so not fair."

"Not fair for the bullies," he laughed. "Now, giddy up, cowgirl."

"You so nasty," Yolo blushed again and dropped the robe.

"Damn, you fine!" he said and came out of the sweats. He climbed on the bed and she climbed on top of him.

"Yee Ha!"

*****

"Hey girl!" Shyne sang as she breezed into her parents' house. She was still floating from an afternoon romp with her husband.

"Hey ya'self, lil' mama," Yolo greeted and hugged her daughter. "You guys take care of your granny while we're away."

"We will. Wish you would have told us you were going to Disney. Muhammad would have wanted to go."

"And do what? He's a year old," she laughed.

"Well, I have an appointment with a doctor anyway," Shyne informed.

"Are you OK? What's wrong?" the mother fussed. She looked her up and down and turned her around to inspect.

"I'm fine, but he's not," she said and showed her a complaint on the 1-800-Killa app.

I'm a gymnast, a really good one, too. I have an excellent shot at the Olympics. I have been seeing our team doctor here in Atlanta and, well, he touches me. Touches me in places I don't need to be touched. He touches himself while he touches me until he grunts. Not just me, he touches all the girls.'

"And I'm about to touch him," Shyne explained.

"Have fun," Yolo beamed happily. They said their goodbyes and headed to the airport. The first stop was Orlando so the kids could have some fun. Afterwards, they could visit Disney. Diedra put on as soon as they reached their hotel.

"I want my own room," Diedra insisted and whipped her hair like the diva she envisioned herself.

"And you'll get your own room. In about twenty years," the father informed. She pouted and crossed her arms over her flat chest.

"Fine!" Diedra relented and marched off.

"Fine!" Yolo teased and laughed. The family went to their reserved suite to put their bags down and have some fun.

"I thought we was going to Disney?" little Killa frowned when his father pulled to a stop at a local park.

"We are. I just wanted to make a quick stop. You guys go play," big Killa said, pointing to the playground. The group of six bullies congregated there to bully smaller kids. It wasn't Disney, but they did like to swing, so they hopped out and traipsed on over.

"Where you going?" Yolo asked when her husband got out of the car.

"To get this footage," he said and pulled his phone to record it.

"Yo, can we get a swing?" little Killa asked as politely as he was able.

"Yo? Where you from?" the head bully asked. He chose him as his next victim, so his followers followed.

"Sounds like a New York boy," a second bully seconded. Actually he was born and bred in Georgia, but raised around New Yorkers and picked up an accent.

"I just want to swing," Diedra said, stepping up to protect her brother. Little Killa knew men are the protectors and maintainers of women, so he stepped forward to protect and maintain his sister.

"You gotta pay to get on these swings," the bully bullied. He extended his hand for payment and got it.

"Or," the five year old said and swung. He caught the much bigger kid on his chin, which dropped him on his ass. His friends moved to jump in the fray and so did Diedra.

"Hayyah!" Diedra shouted and attacked. The seven year old black belt did a spinning back roundhouse kick that knocked a boy clean out. The six was now four. A front kick to the chest dropped a third bully next to the first one. Little Killa and Diedra put their backs together and beat two boys black and blue. A fourth boy ran leaving two. Those two got beat so badly, Killa almost wanted to stop it. Almost, but he was too busy filming.

"Guess it is true. The bigger they are, the harder they fall," Yolo said as she proudly watched her babies beat up the bullies. The bigger boys got enough and ran off. Smaller kids began to clap once the playground was now safe to play once again.

"Guess Disney can wait," Killa said as his kids made new friends and played.Disney waited until the following day, but only one parent got to have fun. The other had to stay in Orlando while the other went to Miami. They settled the issue in a diplomatic fashion.

"Paper, rock, scissors!" Yolo said and threw her hand. It was settled with best out of five and Killa was up.

"Consultation prize?" he asked and dipped under the covers. Yolo replied by spreading her caramel-colored thighs and desert was served.

"Yessss," she hissed as he began to give her a good tongue-lashing. Killa had to grab her hips to hold her in place when she began to thrash and writhe in pleasure. He couldn't prevent her from lifting off the mattress when she began to come. He clamped on and literally sucked one out of her.

"My turn," he said when he rose back uptown. He leaned in at let her lick her own juice from his lips and chin. They locked eyes as he wriggled inside of her and found his stroke. Their tongues danced and darted in each other's mouth while their bodies moved in unison like the electric slide.

"Mmm, get it. Get it all!" Yolo said as another long orgasm crept into her life. She pulled her legs up and open, giving him the green light to take it home.

"I got it," he assured her and picked up his pace. He pounded out a nut for each of them and slumped over spent.

"They don't call you Killa for nothing!" she said, planting grateful kisses all over his mouth and face. They huddled up and drifted off to sleep. Morning came moments later.

"Good morning," Killa greeted when he and Yolo emerged from their bedroom in the suite. Diedra had the other bedroom, while little Killa slept on a roll away bed in the living room.

"Good morning!" the kids sang together before the spokesperson made their appeal.

"We decided we would like waffles before we go to the park," Diedra said at first. "Un uh, those prices are just ridiculous!" Diedra fussed and rolled her eyes when she read the room service menu.

"I know, girl, and you work hard for your money," Yolo said and high-fived her.

"Shole do," she said, then frowned at her daddy. "Where you think you going?"

"I have to run down to Miami real quick. I'll probably be back before you guys leave the park," he assured her.

She seemed to accept the answer while his son couldn't careless. He was going to Disney, so fuck everything else. Yolo took the kids over to the amusement park while, Killa headed to the airport for the shuttle flight south. While he rode it, he gave his beloved a call.

Chapter twenty one

"Hey daddy!" Shyne cheered and waved even though he wouldn't see it over the phone.

"Hey, baby girl," he said and instinctively shot a glance around for Diedra. The child would lose her damn mind if she heard him calling her by the name she claimed as her own. She recently cursed out a stranger at the mall for calling his girlfriend baby girl. Yolo had to start carrying travel size bars of soap to wash her mouth out.

"You must not be with mom," she said, knowingly.

"Nope. Gotta shoot down to Miami and check out these foster parents. What you up to?" he answered and asked.

"I have an appointment with that doctor. The one from the site," she replied. "Gonna try out that new thing."

"Ooh, the 'Feminator-2000?" he asked, greedily rubbing his hands together.

"Yes, sir!" she shot back excitedly. Haneef had been quite busy turning out deadly devices for the upcoming WLM jubilee.

"Well, make sure to turn your body cam is on so we can evaluate it. Wanna make sure it's right before the main event," he relayed.

"I think you just want to see him get fucked up," Shyne said. Her fathers chuckled confirmed her suspicion.

"Mmhm."

"Mmhm, nothing. Anyway, have fun. Love you," he said and sighed.

"Love you more!" she shot back.

Killa didn't believe it because no one could possibly love as hard as he did. He didn't argue though and instead clicked off to board his flight.

*****

Shyne may have had the new 'Feminator-2000', but Killa brought the new 'Python-2000' along with him, a high tech version of a primitive method of death. Not to mention he could travel with it since it looked like a simple sweater. Travel with in his bag that is, because no way he would put that thing on his body. He only had one, so that meant one of the McCoy's would have to get these hands.

"Good morning," Killa's driver said as he slid into the SUV. He nodded at the small bag on the back seat.

"Morning," he replied and leaned back for the ride. The ride ended up in a rundown section of Miami. Killa felt a tug on his heartstrings when he thought about the plight of the nation's children. So many kids get removed from abusive homes only to end up in houses of horror. It was foster homes like this that produced Yolo. They were lucky he came instead of her. Lucky, but still as dead.

"Who is it?" Mrs. McCoy asked as she wobbled up to the door in a moo-moo and scratching her wide ass.

"Exterminator!" he called back and giggled at his own inside joke. A moment later the door opened. It would have stayed closed had he said what he was here to exterminate. They had plenty of mice, roaches and other varmints and vermin, so they welcomed him in.

"'Bout time the landlord sent someone. The foster care people 'sposed to be bringing us another kid," she said, leading the way inside. Killa wasn't sure why he looked down at her large, wide, flat, square butt, but he did.

"Yuck," he grimaced at the sight. He was about to wonder who would marry that until he reached the den and got a gander at Mr. Mc-Coy.

"Who's that, Betty? I know you ain't got no nigga in my house while I'm here?" the one hundred twenty pound man fussed. The question was valid since she would invite black men in their home whenever he went out.

"He's the exterminator," she shot back, but took a longing look up and down the handsome stranger. "Even though I wouldn't mind him putting hands on me!"

"Oh, I'm definitely gonna put my hands on you," Killa mumbled to himself. Playtime was over and out came the gun.

"You fixin' to rob us?" Mr. McCoy asked incredulously. He looked around the sparse house for confirmation and confirmed, "But we ain't got shit!"

"Actually, I'm here to collect what you owe for Jemesha," he growled.

"Bertha? We don't owe that gal nothing! All the rich folks got LNBs and we wanted one, too!" Mrs. McCoy fussed.

"Hold that thought," Killa told her and turned back to him. "Put this on."

"I can't afford no new sweater," he declined until Killa pressed the barrel to his head. He pulled the turtleneck overhead and looked at his cloudy reflection in the dirty mirror. "It's too big."

"It'll shrink a lil," Killa informed and hit the switch. The 'lil' was an understatement. This sweater was going to shrink a lot.

"Um," Mr. McCoy wondered as the sweater tightened around his chest and neck. Every time he let a breath out, it squeezed a little tighter just like its namesake.

"What's going on?" Mrs. McCoy moaned, seeing her husband in distress.

"Well, that's the Python sweater. My man Haneef makes them," he explained as her husband got squeezed to death. His wife watched curiously as he turned red, blue and purple.

Mr. McCoy dropped to the dirty carpet and clawed at the sweater. It was futile since nothing could break its vice like grip. His struggle came to a painful end when the device literally squeezed the life out of him.

"Now..." Killa began as he turned to Mrs. McCoy. She stumped him by dropping her moo-moo, exposing her doughy, puffy rolls of white flesh. He cocked his head curiously and asked, "Huh?"

"I want you to touch me. Put your hands on me!" she pleaded. She walked over and gave the corpse a kick.

"Oh, your gonna get these hands. I promise, but first I need to know all about this WLM. Where are people getting these kids? Who's behind it? Where can I find them!" Killa demanded hotly. This was one of the rare times he lost his cool. The anguish of seeing mothers of missing children haunted the nightly news every night.

"I'on know," she answered with a shrug. That was the wrong answer and he moved in.

The world went completely red as Killa blacked out. He bombarded the large woman with heavy punches to her body and head. The body blows pounded harmlessly into her puffy flesh so he went up top. She tried to run but that too was the wrong answer. Killa clipped her and down she went on her fat face.

"Stop! Help! Stop!" she pleaded as he stomped and kicked recompense out of her.Killa didn't hear a word in his rage. It wasn't until he realized she had left the building that he began to return. He gave a parting kick in her head just for kicks and summoned his ride. While he waited, he searched the house for information on WLM but only found more trash and debris. He left the same bag in the back seat and nodded to the driver when he was dropped back off at the airport. Killa made it back to Orlando before the family left the theme park.

"You OK?" Yolo frowned when she saw remnants of his earlier rage still etched on his face.

"Hmph?" he asked, then shook the anger away and smiled. "They didn't destroy anything did they?"

"So far, so good," she replied. They both smiled as their kids ran from one ride to the next. Both knew they would be there until the park closed. "I wonder how miss Shyne made out?

*****

"Hello?" Mrs. Gross asked curiously when she opened her door to the pretty black woman. Shyne dressed down in athletic apparel and looked like one of the gymnast.

"Is Dr. Gross in?" she asked even though she knew he was because she followed him home.

"So, he's bringing you guys to our home now, I see," she huffed indignantly. Shyne analyzed her and realized she wasn't a party to her husband's crimes.

"No ma'am, I'm the piper," she explained with enough space between the lines. The woman's head nodded as she read the unspoken.

"Well, I guess I'll grab lunch while he pays what he owes. I've been wanting to redo the den," she suggested and grabbed her purse. She gave an appreciative curtsy on her way out.

"Dr. Gross. Oh, Dr. Gross," Shyne sang as she entered the house. The thirsty man heard the sing-song tone of a pubescent girl and came running.

"Huh? Where's Sally?" he asked when he found Shyne in his foyer. She was young, but too old for his taste. His pretty wife was way too old for him, so he never touched her. Then again, she was here, so why not go there.

"She went for lunch, but you're on the plate," Shyne said and pulled her newest weapon.

"What the heck is that?" he asked, leaning his head curiously. The gun looked like an old time pirate weapon with a large opening at the end.

"This, is the Feminator-2000," she explained and paused to read the directions once more.

"What does it do?" he asked in yet another example of 'be careful what you ask for' moment. Shyne lifted one finger, signaling him to wait as she read.

"We need to go your den," she remembered.

"My den? My wife hates that room," he said as he led the way. Once they entered the dated room, he turned and faced his guest.

"Point and shoot," she said and aimed the device at his crotch. She pulled the trigger and a spring-loaded contraption shot out. The steel jaws were like a mini bear trap. They clamped onto his package right through his pants and snatched it completely off. "Yoooooo! That's dope!"

"Hmph?" he asked, trying to make sense of the sights and sounds. A dull pain engulfed him as blood seethed and ran down his legs. He looked at his missing man meat hanging from the steel trap and went to retrieve it.

"Nuh uh," Shyne teased and ran from him. She sang the chase music from Benny Hill as they ran around the room. He slowed as his life's blood left his body and ruined the room. Mrs. Gross was going to get her wish to redecorate the room.

"OK, OK," he sighed and sank to the floor in defeat. He realized more of his blood was on the room's floor than in his body and knew what that meant. He was a doctor after all. That is because his next few breaths would be his last.

"I'll holler!" Shyne said as his troubled soul left its shell. She hit the switch that let his package drop to the floor.

Chapter twenty two

"I'm up next!" Sun firmly declared as the family watched the body cam footage of the Feminator at work. Both he and his father cringed at seeing the man's meat get snatched away.

"That's why it's called the Feminator," Yolo explained when the doctor hit a high note. She shook her head watching her daughter clown around while he chased her for his junk. It reminded her of a similar situation in her youth when she worked for Casper.

"Well, you would hit a falsetto too if someone snatched your jewels and gentiles off," Sun giggled, while his family all shook their heads. They were all known for corny jokes, but Sun was the king.

"Anyway, your up next. Time to try out the 12 Years a Slave," Killa said. They all turned their attention to the screen to see who volunteered to get fucked up next.

Dear 1-800-Killa, I have a problem. My son is some real bullshit. He won't work, won't help out around the house, steals out of my purse and eats up everything in sight. I finally asked him to leave and he put his hands on me. I raised this nasty nigga on my own because his nasty daddy used to put hands on me and now he wanna do the same. Un uh, come kill him. Kill him dead.'

"Twelve years a slave!" the whole family said unison. Young Gutta was lucky the whole family didn't come for him. Paradise is at the feet of mothers and this clown abused his. Now he was about to get his ass whooped in the worst possible way.

*****

"Green's on me tonight!" Gutta cheered and flashed a wad of stolen cash from his mother's tax return. Meanwhile, she was at home nursing a black eye from trying to stop him.

"Hey now!" Tenika sang and winded her narrow hips. She was known in their south Dallas hood to put in work for weed, so Gutta had some head coming his way. She instinctively applied some gloss to her thick lips and stretched her jaws in preparation. She and Gutta were actually cousins, but he had the weed so it didn't matter. Plus, she had the best head in South Dallas, so Gutta didn't care.

"Shit, we may as well skip the club and just get room," he suggested. It would make his ill-gotten gain last a little longer since he couldn't trick it off in one night. Tenika knew it too and nodded her head they same way she did when giving the whole hood head.

"Heck yeah," she said and linked her arm in his. He summoned a cab since he had a little extra dough to blow. Broke people have a tendency to blow every penny they get as soon as they get it. Like they know they're supposed to be broke, so they quickly spend every dime. In a rush to be broke again. Being broke is a mindset, not dollar amount. Even rich people run out of money, but grind to get more. Being broke and being poor are two totally different things.

"Let's get some yack!" the skinny hood rat sang and danced once again.

"Bet," he eagerly agreed for the expensive stuff since he didn't have to work for the money. Plus, she swallowed and that always gets priority. He ignored the condoms behind the counter as he ordered a couple boxes of cigars to roll up. Once they had their party favors, they crossed the street to a rundown motel to party.

"Damn!" Sun said as he followed the condemned man to the motel. It was a wide open drug trap operating at full blast. A young dope boy bust shits at a rival and it didn't raise an eyebrow. Junky chicks turned tricks right there in the parking lot. There was so much going on, no one would pay attention to the screams. "Perfect!"

"First things first!" Gutta said as soon as they entered the room. He was so eager to get inside her mouth he didn't even lock the door behind them. He dropped his jeans and sat back on the bed.

"I know that's right," Tenika giggled and gobbled up his dick.

She knew this was the only thing she was good at and did it good.Gutta tried to roll up while she worked, but had a hard time concentrating. He had to pause when she dipped under his balls and ate the booty like groceries. She expertly tugged at his meat while she tossed his salad. Neither noticed Sun slip in behind them.

"This guy," Yolo said, shaking her head as she and Killa watched the live stream from the body cam. "I'm about to call him and tell him to hurry up!"

"Wait, he got it. Let him handle it," Killa said. Father and Sun both enjoyed watching the show.

"You nasty. Don't expect me to eat ass! I love you to death, but don't even think about it!" she shot back. Meanwhile in Dallas, Gutta reached his destination.

"Come on!" he said urgently and slid back into her mouth. He let out a guttural grunt and added to the semen soup in her belly. This was her fourth dick of the day.

"Mmm," Tenika purred as he pulsed and filled her mouth. Neither heard death ease in and closed the door behind him.

"Shit, you got some good ass head!" he exclaimed and gave her a pat on her head.

"Thank you," she giggled coyly at the only compliment she received these days. She used to hear she had some good puppy until it lost its elasticity. It was still comfortable like an old slipper, but her head was better.

"Sure looked like it was good," Sun said as he stepped forward. He pointed a standard gun in one hand and held the new device in the other.

"Aw mane!" Gutta moaned when he realized he was about to get robbed. He actually felt some kind of way about even though he just stole it from his mama's purse.

"You prolly should leave," Sun told the girl. She swallowed once more to get it all down and stood.

"Sorry cousin, but I gotta go. See you at grandma house," Tenika announced.

"Wait, you just sucked your cousin's dick?" Sun asked incredulously.

"Ate my booty, too. Yeah, we cousins. Been freaking since we was little," Gutta snitched since she was ready to bail on him.

"Better yet, you stay," he decided and rolled out the 12 Years a Slave. It looked like a standard whip until he hit the switch. It lit up the room in an electric blue glow.

"The fuck!" Gutta shouted and backed away. Not far enough though and Sun struck. He twirled the whip in his best slave master imitation and lashed out. "Yeoow!"

"I bet," Sun said as he marveled at the marvelous result of the blow. The electrified whip tore through his clothes, and skin down to the bone. The next strike broke his ribs and revealed his lungs and internal organs. Sun continued to whip him while his cousin cowered in the corner. Each blow tore chunks of skin and bone away. He looked like he had been peeled once he finally collapsed in a mangled heap. Sun found Gutta's pocket in a piece of jeans near the bathroom and collected the stolen money. He almost forgot about the girl until she moved. "Oh yeah? Now what are we gonna do about you?"

"Kill her nasty ass," Yolo huffed from across the country. Luckily for Tenika, her mic wasn't on, so he didn't hear his mother.

"Don't kill me, bruh. I got some fiyah head!" she proclaimed. "Have some?"

"You better not, boy!" Yolo screamed at the monitor. It was unnecessary since Sun immediately declined.

"I'm sure you do, but I'm married. Plus, eww," he grimaced at the thought. Her crimes didn't warrant death, but she did need her ass whooped. He found the piece of Gutta's pants that held his belt and pulled it out.

"Un uh, my daddy ain't even whoop me!" Tenika fussed when she realized what was about to happen.

"That's probably, why, you, turned, out so, fuckd, up!" he said between blows. After giving her a long overdue whooping, he went to return the stolen money.

"Who!" Gutta's mother called out in reply to a knock on her door. There was no answer, so she pulled the door open. She was in more danger inside her home from her raggedy son, so she had no fear of any strangers. "Hmph?"

The woman recognized the piece of her son's expensive jeans since he'd bought them with a stolen paycheck. She could clearly see money sticking out, so she reached down and took it. It was almost what he stole minus weed, cognac, and motel room. She stuffed it in her bra and kicked the piece of bloody jeans off her porch.

*****

"Well, that worked pretty well," Yolo nodded when the show came to an end.

"It did. I can't wait to try out the 'Stroke of un-luck'," he said eagerly.

"Where do you get these names from?" she cracked up. They were too quirky to come from any other source than her husband.

"Um, Haneef makes them up," he lied badly. Yolo knew all his tells and could tell he wasn't telling the truth. He was still going to get some pussy though.

"Would you like some pussy?" she asked cordially. She lifted her hips to remove her panties since he would never say no.

"I could go for a slice," he nodded thoughtfully and slid his pajama pants off.

"My, my," she marveled at his meat. She gave it a kiss, lick and took him inside her warm mouth.

"Flip over," he directed, giving her ass a pat in the direction he wanted her to move. She followed his direction and ended up in the top half of a 69.

He grabbed her pretty buns and leaned up to lick her like she liked.The couple worked separately yet together to please each other. She sucked and stroked while he licked and twirled his tongue around her clit. She was first to lose it and shook from a strong orgasm. Yolo knew another one of her husband's tells and pulled him out of her mouth when his toes curled. One stroke of her hand made her skeet towards the ceiling.

"Ride 'em, cowgirl," Killa slurred when his wife began to mount him.

"Yee haa!" she replied and began to ride.

She rode and wiggled, wiggled and rocked and knocked her mans socks off. Some women will nag, badger, harangue, and harass their man to get their way. Sometimes it works, sometimes it didn't. Yolo on the other hand, fucked her man silly every chance she got and that worked 100% of the time. Chicks could learn a lesson from Yolo. "Yeee Haw!"

Chapter twenty three

"What are you watching and why?" Bryonna asked when she heard a profanity-laced tirade coming the TV. They tried to beep it out, so the TV beeped for a full minute straight. Then the half dressed females charged each other like rams.

"Some reality show. A bunch of washed up rappers and wannabes prostitutes," Sun said and clicked off the TV.

"Thank you. Those people are too much! Got these kids looking up to them and emulating them. Dressing like little thots," she ranted. Being a doctor, she saw the results of kids playing grownup. Teenage pregnancy, drug use as well as STDs were at an all time high.

Sun listened to her anguish and decided to do something about it. Killa's kids didn't do a whole lot of complaining or protesting. They didn't do rallies or speeches. No, they were about that action and he was going to do something.

"Let's go to bed," he urged and guided her up the stairs. He put her to sleep like a good husband does. Once she was snoring, he eased out of bed and got on his computer to do some research. All the offensive reality shows led back to one place. It was so good he had to call his sister and put her on.

"Psst," Shyne hissed at her ringing phone as she danced on the dining room table. Asad picked it up and tossed it aside. Whatever it was had to wait until morning. Because just like the leg bone is connected to the hipbone, a table dance led to some serious boning. The next afternoon the two couples met up for brunch.

*****

"Hey, little man," Bryonna sang as she bounce her nephew on her knee. She was starting to show with her own son taking form in her belly. Sun waited patiently until he had his sister alone and filled her in.

"Yo, you ever watch them reality shows?" he leaned in and asked. "Love and housewives and bullshit."

"You mean the ones where all they do is fight, fuss and fuck? I hate them ratchet shows. Please tell me you wanna kill them! There's one shot right here in Atlanta! We can go over there now and—"

"Hold your horses, ma. I found the person behind all of the shows. Corrupting a whole generation of impressionable kids. We gotta get him," Sun replied.

"Hmph, some rich white man sitting back making millions and laughing at us I bet," Shyne fussed.

"Only half right. He's making millions and he is laughing at the outcome, but it's even worse!" he said.

"Just as dead though," she replied. "Let's try out the 'Stroke of un-luck' on him."

"Let's," Sun agreed. It was easier said than done because now they had to figure out a way to get next to him. They certainly couldn't walk up to his gated mansion. Even the gate couldn't keep his own corruption out.

*****

"Georgette, what do you have on!" Mrs. Denman shrieked when she saw what her 15-year-old daughter was wearing.

"Uh, clothes," she quipped back sarcastically. She took it a step further by rolling her neck and eyes like the little ghetto girl she was not. "Um, I saw a chick on one of my father's shows wearing it, so stop sweating me. Talk to the hand!"

"George!" Mrs. Denman called and set out in search of her husband. "George!"

"Ish!" he fussed and quickly clicked away from the screen he was on.

He had an idea for a new show and didn't want anyone to see it un-til it was ready. He'd noticed how well people responded to colorful homosexuals, so he made sure to include one on each of his reality shows.

A brainstorm during a blowjob sparked an idea to create a reality show of colorful homosexuals. He dubbed it Fuckmen and recruited fuckmen from all over the country. Of course he started with the fuckman on his knees in front of him. He wouldn't have promoted homosexuality if he wasn't a fuckman himself.

"Come talk to your daughter! She's been watching your shows again!" Mrs. Denman snapped at her husband.

"Oh no!" he reeled and hopped to his feet. Even he knew how detrimental his content was and shielded his own child from it. They marched into her room and found her practicing giving head on a piece of produce.

"Ugh!" she fussed before removing the cucumber from her larynx. "Don't fucking barge into my room!"

"Girl, what are you doing?" her mother wondered, but not her father. He signed off on the episode featuring a man teaching women how to please a man.

"Ju-Ju taught how to suck a di—"

"Georgette, how many times did we tell you not to watch those shows! They are for common black folk!" he said like the bougie black folk that he was.

"But all the kids at my school watch it! They all dress like it and talk like it!" she said since black people can be the biggest followers on the planet. Let someone deemed to be cool declare something, anything as cool and they flock to it like zombies to loud noises. Black America was turning into an episode of the walking dead. It's hard to stay woke when you're brain dead.

"Well, fuck them kids," he let slip then caught himself. "I mean, um, I'll make a deal with you. No watching my shows and I'll buy you a pony?"

"I'd rather have butt shots like the girl on the California show!" she insisted. It was a stroke of pure karma that his own child was just as corrupted as the masses and it was all his fault. That could have been punishment enough, but Sun and Shyne were on the way. Bad to worse if ever there was one.

*****

"Nice crib!" Shyne admired when she and Sun drove by George's spread. The surveillance was designed to find a way in but it wouldn't be easy. "I almost hate to burn it down."

"No you don't," Sun laughed. They carefully scanned the block and neighborhood as they drove through. They would switch cars and come back again so they didn't draw attention.

"Look at it!" Shyne said when a landscaping crew pulled to one of the fancy houses. A honk on the horn granted them instant access.

"That's our way in," he agreed. It would have been easier to ask their father but they wanted to handle it on their own. He was his father's son and would figure it out.

It took a few days until he put together a truck and trailer to look like a landscape crew. They waited until Georgette left for school with her mother so they would be safe. Georgette needed her butt whipped not dead. Her mother got nowhere with the girl who insisted looking like a little thot just like her new role models. Maybe mourning would snap her out of it.

"How I look?" Shyne asked as they pulled up to the gate.

"Like Speedy Gonzalez," he laughed. "Why you dressed like a Mexican?"

"Duh, we're supposed to be landscapers!" she shot back.

"Yo, that's so racist!" he said, shaking his head and rang the bell.

"On a Tuesday?" George frowned when he answered the buzz at the gate. His lawn looked great, but he shrugged and buzzed them in. With one button he let death into his life.

"We're in!" Shyne cheered as they pulled in. She and Sun rolled their rented equipment off and started them up. The sound of the lawnmower and weed eater drowned out the sound of Sun kicking in the front door.

"Hmph?" George asked curiously. He left his gay porn on the screen and went to investigate. "Who are you? Why are you in my home?"

"I'm the piper and it's time to pay up," Shyne snared in a sinister tone.

"Yo, is that what you be saying?" Sun cracked up.

"Yeah! Then when I'm about to send them off I hit 'em with, 'I'll holler!' It's dope!" she explained.

"It's whack! It's like cruel and unusual punishment. The last thing someone hears is some corny crap like that!" he shot back.

"Um, excuse me," George interjected. "Who are you? Why are you in my home?"

"We're Killa's kids and we're here to kill you!" Sun growled at him and turned back to his sister. "See, that's how it done!"

"We're Killa's kids, here to kill you. That's so whack!" Shyne mocked. She turned back to George to get his opinion. "Bruh, what would you rather hear before you die? Something witty like 'pay the piper' or something scary like 'Killa's kids' here to kill you?"

"I'm calling the police!" George said and turned to make good on his threat.

"No you're not," Sun replied and hit him with the 'Stroke of un-luck'. The modified tranquilizer gun fired a dart into his backside.

"Ooowee," he moaned from the sting of the dart. He felt the effects of the liquid entering his body immediately. "What did you give me?"

"Just a massive dose of sodium. Feel your blood pressure rising?" Sun asked. "We should have called it 'Pressure bust pipes', but my dad, he comes up with the names."

"I—I do?" he replied as his vision blurred and his head began to pound. Soon blood vessels began to burst from the pressure. Shyne went to work while the drug did its job.

"Oh, wow!" she exclaimed when she began to browse through his computer. It was chock full of deliberate corruption and vice. George and his partners researched the affects of their shows and knew it damaged youth. It also paid well so they decided, 'fuck them kids'. She shared the files as well as his secret sex life with all the gossip shows.

"This dude is a real creep!" Shyne snarled when she returned.

"Was," Sun corrected as George seized from a massive stroke. He tried to beg for help but words were beyond his grasp. Death was closer and closed in and embraced him.

"I'll holler," Shyne leaned in with a whisper and a giggled. Sun just shook his head and led the way out. George's death wouldn't put an end to the destructive and unrealistic reality shows but it made the twins happy. They happily high-fived and skipped happily away.

*****

"Man, look at that shit!" Shyne fussed as they drove by a police stop on the way home. The routine stop quickly turned into a routine ass whooping when the young black man mouthed off to the cop.

"What you stopping me for!" he hopped out and demanded in the cops face. He knew he was pulled over for being black, but that was the wrong way to handle it. Some of these racist cops were dying to get a notch on their belts. Especially since they never got convicted.

"Ooh!" Sun grimaced when the cop replied by scooping him up and slamming him on his head. "Pull over!"

"Yo, we can't get him now. Body cams, surveillance cams and too many witnesses," Shyne complained but complied. They joined the spectators who recorded the spectacle on their phones.

"Shit!" the cop fussed when he saw all the people catching the beat down. He could care less about being on the news since nothing would happen to him. He was just upset he didn't get to kill him before all the witnesses showed up. He had to settle for locking him up for assault on a police officer. Sun and Shyne had to settle for his name and badge number so they could catch up with him later.

Chapter twenty four

"How's about a little loving before I go to work?" Lamont asked and raised his eyebrows in an attempt to be sexy.

It was a valid question since he was about to drive an hour to work 12 hours before he could turn around and drive another hour back home. He had to do this six days a week to take care of his new wife Kim.

He was so grateful that a regular guy like him could pull a bad chick like Kim. She was expensive, but he was totally in love. He worked like a slave to keep her hair and nails done weekly. Then she needed clothes and shoes and since she was all dressed up she needed to go to the club as well. If he had any complaints it would be lack of sex. He would like to visit her vagina every now and again.

"I got my period again," she quickly dismissed. If she had one complaint, it would be having to have sex with him occasionally. He did finance her comfortable life and that was her contribution.

"Again?" he reeled since he knew her period just ended. He kept tabs on it because he was ready to be a father. That of course required they have sex sometime. It had been months since she parted with some pussy.

"Yeah, well. Un huh," she said since she really didn't feel like she owed him an explanation. In fact she felt like he owed her since she was clearly out of his league. She was light skin and pretty and he was brown and plain. She was doing him a favor by allowing him to take care of her. "Well, go on to work. You don't want to be late,"

"Um, OK," he sighed sadly. He leaned in for some sugar but only got salt when she turned her face and gave him cheek to kiss. Pretty much the same as giving him her ass to kiss.

"Yeah and don't forget to ask about picking up a few more shifts. I'll need a lot of cash for my cruise," she reminded.

"You sure you don't want me to come? It'll be so romantic," he offered once again.

"It's a girls trip, duh," she said curtly and escorted him to the door. She practically pushed him out of his house and closed the door.

"Hello, Mrs. Martin," Lamont waved to his elderly neighbor who was watering her flowers.

"Mm hm," she said like she always did. The old lady kept her lips pressed tight whenever she saw him so the truth wouldn't fall out. She was old school and tried to mind her business as much as possible.

"Well, OK. Have a nice day, Mrs. Martin," he said and jumped into his car. She watched him pull off and bend the corner out of sight. She turned her head to the next corner just in time to see another car come around and pull into the driveway.

"Hello, ma'am," the tall, pretty boy greeted her like he did every morning when he came over.

"Fuck you!" she shot back and shot him the middle finger just in case he didn't hear well. It was the same greeting she greeted him with every morning. She despised him and his adulterous girlfriend Kim.

"No, thank you. Too old. I'm about to go in here and beat this young pussy up!" he laughed and hooked his thumb towards the house just as the front door began to open.

"Hello, Mrs. Martin!" Kim called and waved to her neighbor as she held the door open wide for her boyfriend. Not as wide as she was about to hold her legs though.

"Fuck you, too!" she said emphatically. Kim and her friend laughed at her and disappeared behind the door. Mrs. Martin knew what they were going to do so she went to file a formal complaint.

"Come on, Brad. We gonna do it right here!" Kim demanded and pulled him on the sofa. She was so horny she couldn't make it to the bedroom.

"Let me see how bad you want it!" he dared as she fumbled with his zipper. He was semi erect by the time she freed him from his pants.

She wanted it plenty and swallowed it almost to the hilt. She worked her head, lips and tongue until she had a full-fledged erection in her mouth.

Brad reached down and played in her pussy until he had a puddle. He pulled out her mouth and pushed her back onto her back. She pulled her legs wide like she did the door that let the man into her husbands house and let the man into her husband's vagina. He snatched her by the ankles and beat the box up like a disgruntled UPS driver.

"Let me get that!" Kim demanded when Brad's face began to contort in pleasure. Her husband wanted a baby so bad she was going to give him one. It just wouldn't be his. Brad let her get it all right and leaned in and bust on her cervix.

*****

"And that's some real bullshit!" Shyne grumbled when she read Mrs. Martin's report. She took the extra step and uploaded footage from her security camera. It showed Lamont leaving for work and Brad pulling in moments later.

"What baby?" Asad asked when he heard his wife grumble. Shyne took such good care of him that he jumped to please her as well. It's true a happy wife leads to a happy life.

"Nothing I can't handle!" she said and hurried to click away from the 1-800-Killa site.

"OK," he said and shrugged.

"But I do have something I need your help with," she pleaded. He opened his mouth to ask what but she already stepped out of the tiny shorts she wore around the house.

"I'm sure I can handle that!" he assured her and scooped her up. He carried her over to the bed and handled that.

"Works every time," Shyne giggled to herself as she eased out of bed. She checked on her son who was sleeping soundly as well courtesy of a full belly. "Works every time."

Shyne went back to the computer to finish research on officer 'bust a nigga head.' Officer Alston liked beating up black men so he was going to get a taste of his own medicine. She discovered he had a freaky fetish that was going to get him fucked up. The GPS tracker she put on his car put him at the same massage parlor everyday before his shift. D.N.G was a discrete all male massage parlor that only massaged one part of a man. They specialized in hand jobs, hence their name D.N.G, an acronym for damn near gay.

"Oh, you all the way gay!" Shyne said with a grimace when she read the mission statement on the website. They provided a service where gay curious men to give and receive hand jobs. No Damn near about it.

*****

"One, two, three...shoot!" Sun called as he and Shyne settled who got to get the crooked cop. He was really about to be crooked because Shyne won.

"Yes!" Shyne cheered as she won the best two out of three. She did a happy dance at getting to be the one to straighten the crooked cop. It was a cross between the shuffle, electric slide and the bus stop.

"Yeah, you got me," Sun conceded a little too easily for Shyne. She twisted her lips and scrunched her face dubiously.

"What you got going on, homie?" she demanded when it dawned on her. She had never been able to beat him that easily in life.

"I'm not going no where near D.N.G cuz I ain't no where near gay," he explained. That was the best place to catch the cop with his pants down, and he wanted no parts of it.

"Well, actually you will still need to infiltrate the place. Just give a few hand jobs and gather informa—Ma! Mommy!" Shyne yelled and took off when her brother came after her. "Ma! Get yo son!"

"I'm gonna give you a hand job around your neck!" he vowed and gave chase.

"You hear your daughter?" Killa asked when the screams reached them in the kitchen. They were coupled with laughter so they knew it wasn't serious.

"Knowing her, she said or did something crazy and deserve whatever he does to her," Yolo huffed.

Shyne ran throughout the house singing her Benny Hill music and cracking everyone up. He caught up with her in the den and tackled her. Naturally, Diedra jumped in to help her big sister while little Killa joined in to help Sun. Grandma Diedra couldn't help but to steal a few free licks on everyone. Asad had to hold the baby back from joining in while Bryonna just shook her head. It was a typical weekend with the Killa clan to be followed by a typical brutal murder by Killa's kids.

*****

"Uggh!" Sun fussed to himself as he approached the door of D.N.G. Shyne was right and he had to gain access to the all male spot so he could let his sister in before Alston arrived for his daily hand job from a man. It was affectionately called a man job. That's why Shyne was bringing the feminator 2000. These dudes wanted to act like chicks so she would turn them into chicks.

"Are you here for a man job?" the perky receptionist greeted as he came through the door.

"Nope," he replied and fired a dart. Technically tranquilizer darts should be placed in meaty areas like a flank or backside. Sun decided to put in his throat just for kicks. Sun went room to room tranquilizing both staff and clients. Everyone got tied up but anyone with a wedding band got photographed on their own phones and sent to their wives. A woman has a need and a right to know if her husband is damn near gay. And getting a man job is plenty gay.

"You straight?" Shyne asked as she entered the parlor in response.

"Yeah, but I'm the only one! Go look in the storeroom," he exclaimed. Shyne frowned curiously and went to check out the prisoners.

"Oh my!" she reeled when she saw all the men of all races and walks of life bound and gagged. There were bankers, teachers, insurance salesmen, and a couple of urban authors and publishers. Oh my, is right.

"A yo!" Sun called when he spotted the cop approaching the front door. He checked the press on mustache and large glasses he wore as disguise and greeted Alston.

"Welcome to um, oh, D.N.G. What can we get for you today?"

"Let me have a man job. Wanna relieve a little stress before my shift," he explained to convince himself.

"Sure, room two," Sun said pointing down the hall. "Strip down and someone will be right in."

Alston nodded and walked down the hall. He entered the room and stripped out of his uniform. He lay on the bed and waited for the man job that wasn't coming. Instead the door opened and Shyne rushed in aiming the Feminator 2000.

"You're a girl!" Alston fussed and hopped off the table.

"So are you!" Shyne said with a sinister giggled and fired the device. The steel jaws shot out and bit off his junk in one bite. Sun was right behind her aiming a traditional weapon. He paused a split second before erasing his face with the 40 caliber to let him feel the pain.

The cop's mouth opened wide, but no sound came out. The decibel level was so high, it couldn't be heard by human ears. He could only point at his missing meat with one hand while clutching his empty groan with the other.

"WLM!" Sun said, reading the tattoo on his chest a split second before shooting. The tattoo gave him an even better idea. "Call an ambulance for him!"

"What? Why save him?" Shyne reeled with his man meat still hanging from the device.

"Save her, you mean," he laughed as Alston gripped his middle trying to keep his blood in his body.

"OK, but he's not getting this back," she pouted. They called an ambulance who could save his life but not his masculinity. He would be forever feminated. "I'll holler, Bruce Jenner!"

Chapter twenty five

"Ooh, we should take this one! I love adulterers!" Yolo cheered, meaning she loved to kill them.

"Remember the last ones?" Killa fondly recalled the time they stoned couple of adulterers. "We got biblical with that one."

"Um, I was the first one to take the report, so this one is mine!" Shyne insisted. The family had an unspoken rule of first come, first served.

"I want in, though. I feel bad for Lamont. Working like a dog and that nasty broad bringing dudes in his house," Sun said wistfully.

"Well, the both of you go. You can try out the 'Chill-out,'" Killa said firmly. That had long been his approach anytime the twins argued about who got to do what. He made them acquiesce and do it together.

"Bruh, no. We gotta figure out a better name than that!" Yolo insisted.

"Ok babe," Killa said and immediately threw his hands up to let her have her way. Sun squinted at him, but held his questions for later.

"What exactly does it do?" Shyne asked, ready to come up with new name for the new device.

"It sprays liquid nitrogen. Freezes anything it comes in contact with instantly," he explained.

"Ooh! We used that in school! Froze a tennis ball and it shattered like glass!" Sun cheered way too excitedly.

"And I'm gonna freeze that philandering pretty boy's balls," Shyne vowed.

"Ball buster," Yolo tossed out and nodded. The kids didn't feel it, but Killa nodded along with his wife.

"Ball buster it is!" Killa proclaimed and that was the end of it. "Remember the WLM jamboree is in a few weeks so be ready."

"Grrr," Sun and Shyne replied. The meeting was adjourned and they split up. Shyne and Yolo stepped into the kitchen while Sun pursed his lips and cocked his head curiously at his father.

"What?" Killa asked, seeing something was on his mind. He mentally braced himself to impart some good fatherly advice.

"Nothing, its just, I noticed that—bruh, you whipped! Mom always, always gets her way. Always!" he asked, straining to understand why a man let's his wife win all the time.

"Oh, that's simple. I let her have her way because she got a vagina. That trumps being right. Fuck being right!" he explained and he was right.

*****

"Mm-mm-mph!" Kim moaned and arched her back even more. A perfect position for back shots, but works pretty good to get ate out from the back, as well. Brad grabbed a round ass cheek in each hand and peeled the booty open and dug in. Kim shrieked and had the best orgasm of her life. Ironic, really, since it would be her last.

"My turn!" Brad cheered triumphantly at his handiwork when she collapsed and shivered on her husband's bed. All she could do was roll over and open her mouth.

"Aaaaah," Kim said as she opened wide. Wide enough for Brad to slide his man in her mouth and fuck her face. Sun and Shyne had eased into the back door and had seen enough. They began to pop out of their hiding spot, but the bedroom door suddenly burst open.

"I knew it!" Lamont screeched like a wounded animal when he ran in on his wife with her mouth full of man meat. "I knew it! I knew it!"

"What is he doing here?" Brad asked, still stroking her face. She of course couldn't answer because her mouth was full.

"What am I doing here?" Lamont growled as he raised his gun. The huge barrel convinced Brad that now would be a good time to take his dick out of her mouth.

"Why aren't you at work!" Kim shouted as she spit the dick out and popped up. She shouted and got shot because Lamont aimed at her tonsils and fired.

"Oh shit!" Brad freaked out when the bullet, blood, and brains flew out the hole in the back of her head.

"Uh oh," Shyne whispered from the shadows. She would hate to have to kill the victim, but it was getting sketchy.

"Wait," Sun said and waited to see how it played out. He gripped his own gun tightly and waited.

"Chill, Lamont. I didn't know she was married! She said she was divorced!" Brad pleaded with his hands up.

"Which is it? And how you know my name?" Lamont asked as he inched closer, pointing the gun.

"Uh oh," Shyne repeated when she realized he was getting to close. He found out the hard way when Brad lunged for the gun. It fired wildly as they began to struggle for control. A bullet barely missed the twins, so Sun made his move.

"Freeze!" Sun said as he popped out and fired the device. A spray of liquid nitrogen instantly froze Brad's neck. Lamont snatched the gun and turned to see Sun's gun pointed in his face.

"Who are you? And you? Wow, this chick had everyone in my house! " he asked when Shyne stepped out from behind him. He shook his head in disparity as he raised his gun to his own temple. "It don't matter. I'm going to jail anyway."

"Wait!" Sun shouted to stop him. Brad stood there trying to figure out what happened to him when he couldn't speak or breath. "Give me the gun!"Lamont reluctantly handed it over. Sun immediately fired a round into Brad's frozen throat. It shattered like glass and he dropped dead next to the adulteress.

"What about me?" Lamont asked curiously. He drove home with the intention to die or go to jail today.

Sun responded by shooting him in his shoulder, leg, and one more flesh wound in his side. Wounds that definitely couldn't be self inflicted. He then put the gun in Brad's hand.

"He broke into your back door while you and your wife were in bed," Shyne explained as she slid the phone across the floor to him. "You don't remember anything else."

"I don't remember anything else," he repeated and nodded. He watched the killers leave and called 911 to report the intruder.

*****

"Oh wow!" Yolo exclaimed when Shyne filled her in on the botched mission.

"Yeah, mommy. It was crazy, but it worked," she said. The news reported that an intruder was killed after breaking in and attacking a couple in their home. The lead detective didn't buy it 100%, but didn't care much for adulterers either, so he closed the case.

"Y'all dodged a bullet," she said, shaking her head at the wild story.

"We dodged a few bullets," Shyne corrected. She paused for moment to recall Lamont shooting wildly when Brad attacked. "Anyway, what's next?"

"Her," Yolo said showing a picture on her social media feed. Shyne leaned in and scrunched her face up at the rich, white chick holding a little black baby.

"That kid ain't mixed," Shyne said and read the hashtag #LNB "Grrr."

"Grrr is right. Pack a bag. We're going back to Cali," her mother replied. Yolo tried, but just couldn't stop herself from singing the song by the late great B.I.G. "Going back, back to Cali, Cali..."

"Who is that? M.C. Hammer?" Shyne asked curiously and seriously. "Daddy! Dad!"

"I got your M.C. Hammer!" Yolo said as she chased her daughter. Anyone confusing the classic MC with the rapper deserved what they got.

"What now?" Killa asked as his daughter tried to hide behind him.

"She called Biggie, Hammer!" the mother snitched.

"What!" he reeled and stepped aside. Shyne needed her butt kicked for mixing them up. Luckily for her, she was a lot younger and a little quicker and managed to get away. She ran out the house, jumped in her car and took off.

*****

"MC Hammer," Yolo said, still shaking her head when she and Shyne met up at the airport. Shyne wisely brought her son with her to distract her mother. Christi absolutely insisted she bring her when she told her they were coming out to the west coast.

"Well, that's before my time. You guys had it good with Rakim, U.G.K., Biggie, and Outkast. Now, all we got is cross dressing mumble rappers," Shyne fussed with an appropriate amount of disgust on her face.

"Well baby, your generation is a lot gayer than ours. It was a different time. We didn't need no welfare state. Everybody pulled their weight. Boy, our old LaSalle ran a great—"

"Those were the days!" a bystander who was standing to close chimed in and sang. Yolo cracked up, but Shyne was still too young to get it.

"You old people," Shyne said and shook her head as her mother and the stranger began singing the theme song to *Good Times*.

They had to do something to entertain themselves during the long ass line to clear airport security. Shyne had her toddler to keep her busy until they made it up to the screeners. A commotion caught everyone's attention as a Muslim man was removed from line to be deported.

"Didn't we send you back to Yemen once already!" the TSA supervisor barked.

"Yes, you did, but I'm American! My name is Sa'id Salaam. I'm from the Bronx!"

"Get him out of here," Yolo cosigned and cracked up, with her instigating ass. They boarded their own plane for long, cross-country flight.

*****

"I can't believe you actually decided to hang out with me!" Sun said when he and his brother and brother-in-law arrived at a mall. Shyne and his son were off to California, so he agreed to help Sun pick out a gift for Bryonna.

"Please, don't make me regret it," Asad sighed. If he had a dollar for every time Sun or even Shyne nutted up in a mall when they were growing up, he'd have quite a few dollars.

"Bruh, have I ever—never mind," he said, catching himself before telling a lie. He shrugged and said a silent prayer as they entered the mall. There was a moment of silence since Asad was praying, too.

"It's always busy this time of year," Asad groaned when he saw the throngs of Christmas shoppers.

"I should have bought a helmet," Sun laughed when a fight between two women broke out over the hottest, must have toy.

"Whoop her ass, mama!" a little girl cheered. She wanted that toy bad enough to jump in the fray. The other woman's two kids jumped in and it was a free for all.

"Should we do something?" the good Samaritan Asad, asked.

"Definitely!" Sun agreed and pulled his phone to record it. That's all they were getting out of him. He had plenty of footage by the time security managed to break up the fight. They turned and headed into the bowels of the mall in search of something special for his special woman.

"I don't wanna see Santa Claus," a little girl grimaced and shook her head vigorously.

"Why not? It's Santa Claus?" her mother reeled. The child was all excited last week, but this week wore a mini mask of disgust.

"He nasty!" she said, unable to explain why. The dirty man had her feeling dirty by the time she got off his lap. The mother shrugged it off, but Asad was curious.Sun dipped into a jewelry store to add to his wife's collection while Asad ambled over to the North Pole display. He immediately became suspicious of the rented Santa Claus. His shifty eyes kept shifting over all the children. Asad noticed one of his arms was fake while he used the other to hold children on his lap. He concealed his other arm under his costume and jacked off.

"Grrrr," Asad said and attacked. He rushed over and snatched Santa off his Santa chair and slammed him on his Santa head. The local news happened to be on sight and caught the whole thing in high definition.

"Break it up!" mall cops shouted as they moved in. Asad stomped the man until he was tackled and cuffed.

"I want him arrested! Look what he did to me!" the fake Santa demanded and drew attention to his fake arm. All faces frowned and waited for an explanation. He had one and took off running. Sun pulled his camera again and recorded the rent-a-cops chasing the rented Santa. They caught up with him and took both him and Asad to the mall cop station. A check of both names revealed a law-abiding citizen and the other wanted on charges of child molestation.

"You're free to go," Asad was told and un-cuffed. The real cops took the lumped up Santa away when they arrived.

"And you was telling me not to make you regret it," Sun chided.

Chapter twenty six

"We're back, back in Cali, Cali..." Yolo rapped as they made their way through LAX. She side eyed her daughter, daring her to say MC Hammer again. But Shyne had Googled it on the flight and was up to speed.

"Cali got gun play, models on the runway," she joined and rapped along with her mom. They were on the next song from *Ready To Die* when they were spotted walking through the airport.

"Mom! Shyne!" Christi sang and ran over to hug her family. The family had a touching reunion before collecting their bags to head over to Christi's house.

"What's that about?" Shyne decided to ask when they spotted a third white woman sporting a little black baby like a purse.

"I'on know. It's like a trend now. I keep seeing it lately. Even Ashley Evens has one," Christi replied.

Yolo and Shyne shared a quick conspiring glance when they heard the famous name they were here to see. No one knows exactly what she was supposed to be famous for since she didn't sing or act. She did have a few sex tapes with other celebrities. But this was the age of being famous just for being famous and now she was rich and famous as a result.

"Anyway, I hear you guys have some pretty good chicken and waffles out here?" Yolo said, changing the subject to her third favorite subject. Fucking her husband was number one, closely followed by giving bad people bad ends. After that she loved to eat.

"You mean Roscoe's?" Christi replied, assuming she meant the iconic eatery.

"Un uh! S and S chicken and waffles just opened out here, too. They're everywhere!" Shyne cosigned.

"Cuz, them shits are delicious!" Yolo added and ended the shameless plug. The ladies and little Muhammad set off to stuff their faces.

After that it was time to stuff Ashley's face. She was an airhead, so they brought their latest device the 'Air-head' along to try out.

*****

The ladies settled in at Christi's house to relax. They turned on the news to get caught up. After hearing the good, bad and ugly of Los Angeles, the news turned national.

'In other news, a mall Santa got his ass whipped in Atlanta. Police were called in response to the incident.'

"Is that Asad?" Christi asked and blinked rapidly at the TV. Shyne squinted and moved forward despite it being a 65" 4k, super high definition television.

"Um, nope. That's not my husband. Un uh, don't look nothing like him," she replied.

"Abbi! Daddy!" little Muhammad said, pointing at his father on TV slamming Santa on his head. The little boy cracked up while Shyne eased away and pulled out her phone.

"As salaamu alaykum habibati," Asad greeted, meaning peace unto you, my beloved. That was his pet name for his beloved wife and she called him daddy unless her real daddy was around.

"Don't habibati me! Why are you on TV slamming Santa Claus on his head?" she pleaded.

"Um, cuz?" he shrugged. The news reporter came to his defense when they explained he was a wanted sex offender. Shyne twisted her lips and listened to the rest of the story. They untwisted by the end of the report.

"Well, I guess you get a pass. That's a good deed, so I'll email you a coochie coupon. You can redeem it as soon as I get home."

"Oh, I am going to redeem it as soon as you get home!" he assured her.

"Wanna see it?" she whispered wickedly and slipped into the bathroom.

"Un huh. Let me see it," he agreed despite having literally hundreds of pictures of her vagina.

Vagina is one of those things you can never have enough pictures of. Like sunsets and exotic cars and kittens. Shyne stripped from the waist down and took some glamour shots of her kitty cat. Asad was still too reserved and slightly shy and rarely sent any back. That was fine by Shyne since she knew that modesty is an intrinsic part of Islam. Besides, she took plenty of pictures of him when he was sleep, so she had her own collection. Being naughty turned her on, so she went ahead and rubbed one out for the both of them. She stifled a screech when she reached her destination and came back out.

"Really?" Yolo asked and laughed. Come to find out she didn't stifle the screech as well as she thought.

"Yup," Shyne said and shrugged. She read her mothers diary so what could she say. Yolo knew she read her diary and couldn't say nothing. She inherited her freakiness just like her curly hair and her father's golden colored eyes.

*****

"I hate to leave you guys, but I have some follow-ups to do," Christi explained as she prepared for work the next morning.

"We understand. Do what you have to do. We'll find something to do," Shyne sighed even though she knew exactly what they had planned for the day.

"Yeah, I wanna take one of those Hollywood tours. See the stars," Yolo added enthusiastically.

"Ma, if you wanna see stars, just look up. I despise these so-called stars people look up to. How you special because you can play make believe?" Christi fussed.

She had a right too since she had to deal with the results of their corruption. She had to treat the STDs, the unwanted teen pregnancies, and rape of young girls literally dying to be bad girls, real housewives and hip hop chicks. "They need their asses kicked. Some of them need to be dead!"

"Well, yeah," Yolo agreed since she knew what was coming. At least one of them would be dead by the end of the day.

"Look at big sis all mad! Grrr," Shyne teased.

"Yeah, well anyway, you guys have fun. I'll be home around three, God willing," Christi advised. She hugged and kissed her mom, sister and nephew and set off to work.

"Well, let's go shoot a star," Shyne snickered. "Get it? Shoot, star? Shooting stars."

"You are your father's daughter," Yolo nodded. They hopped in Christi's spare car and set off for Hollywood. They had to make a quick pit stop through the hood first though.

"As salaamu alaykum," family friend Jlihd greeted as he met the ladies.

"Was alaykum as salaam," Yolo and Shyne greeted in unison.

"How's my brother?" he asked as he held the door open so the ladies could exit the car. They followed him over to the loaner he provided for the day. It was fully equipped with all the bells, whistles and guns they needed for their outing.

"Crazy as ever. Give him a call. I'm sure he'd love to hear from you," Yolo advised and thanked him for the weapons and car.

"I will," he nodded and turned immediately, calling Killa to check on them. It's so important to keep tabs on loved ones. It sucks logging onto to social media and seeing RIP's for people you love, yet haven't been in touch with. Rest in peace, Sherrod Forrest.

"Can't wait to try this out," Shyne said when she dug in the bag and found the super charged air compressor they dubbed the 'air head'.

It was a remake of the weapon Yolo used when she reached her goal of one hundred before twenty-one. A goal Shyne missed by a mile. She was a beast in her own right, but couldn't hold a candle to the lovely little lunatic.

"Well, you about to," her mother replied. They rode over to Hollywood where Yolo and Muhammad boarded a guided tour bus. Shyne followed in the loaner and listened to the tour guide narrate as they rode.

"And now we're coming up to the mansion once owned by Cher until Ashley Evens purchased it last year. She, of course, made her claim to fame by, um?" the tour guide paused to check her tour guides guide. but it didn't have any information either. She shrugged and moved on to the next house.

"Sho nuff," Shyne giggled when she saw the gate to Ashley's estate was wide open.

Being young and dumb meant life was one long party, so it was rarely closed.

Shyne cautiously pulled in and rolled down the driveway. She parked next to a brand new Bentley and looked around before stepping out. A pair a someone's panties hung over a security camera above the door, but Shyne still donned her disguise for any others or witnesses. The wig and large shades were plenty to obscure her features.

"Bad girls move in silence and violence," Shyne rapped quietly as she eased into the unlocked front door. The remnants of several drugs still hung in the air along with the aroma of a recent orgy.

Shyne was already on a murder mission, but she found the woman's pet child in a doggie cage she got mad. Growling mad when the little boy stuck his little hand out for a handout.

Shyne knew it would be dangerous for him to be free until she finished, so she picked up a piece of a cold pizza from a box and handed it to him. She felt her heart break seeing him devour the food.

"Grrr," Shyne growled as she set out in search of Ashley. She gripped the concentrated air compressor as she started up the circular stairs.

"Smoke?" a stoner type asked when he passed Shyne in the hall. She got to try out the device and aimed at his face. A powerful burst of air entered his nostril and blew a large piece of his skull out the back. "I don't smoke."

Sounds of sex directed Shyne toward the end of the hall. Ashley had no shame in her game and was having sex with a guy and didn't even know his name. The young black man had her bent over and was beating her back out while smoking. Shyne aimed at his tattooed back and blew a hole clean through him.

"Cool!" the man said, watching the weed smoke billow out his chest. It wasn't cool when the pain caught up to and he fell over dead.

"What the hell are you doing!" Ashley demanded in a rage. "He almost made me cum and you killed him!"

"Yeah and now—wait, your more concerned about missing a nut? Not the dead guy on your back? Not the hungry kid in a dog cage? Not the dead guy in the hall?"

"No, no and no! I was right there!" she fussed. Fussed and got completely fucked up. Shyne put the air compressor down and picked up her fist.

"Now, your about to go bye-bye," Shyne grunted and attacked. The beating began with hands and feet, but ended with her beating her with everything she could get her hands on. A large dildo caught her eye and sparked idea.

"Ugh!" Ashley grunted and gagged when Shyne shoved it down her throat.

The woman was used to deep throating, but Shyne put her body weight on it until half her hand was in her mouth. Her arms and legs flailed, but failed to dislodge the rubber dick from her larynx.

"Go to the light, Carol Ann!" Shyne urged as she struggled to hold on to her wasted life. Ashley seemed to nod slightly and she let go. "I'll holler!"

Shyne paused when she went back down and tried to figure out what to do the black kid. She let him out and he reached for another piece of cold pizza. She gave him a slice and took him with her to the car.

*****

"Whose kid?" Christi asked when she returned home to find a new addition.

"She found it on the side of the road," Yolo replied and shook her head once again.

She would have put him back in his little cage and called authorities to come find the scene. Shyne had a good reason since police would have responded in seconds in that neighborhood. She wouldn't have made it out the doorway before the cops came knocking.

"Really, mom?" Christi said, shaking her own head as she scooped the child up.

"Keep him," Shyne suggested. "You and your partner will make great moms."

"Well I don't know if I—wait, what?" Christi frowned when the words finished processing. "You think I'm a lesbian?"

"Well, you don't have a man. I can't remember you ever having a boyfriend," Yolo added softly. "Not judging. I, um, we don't love you any less."

"I am not gay! What's wrong with you people?" Christi reeled. "Didn't you raise me to keep chaste until I get married?"

"Yeah, but," Yolo replied and twisted her lips.

"These guys these days don't want a relationship or marriage. They wanna fuck something," she shot back.

"Shole do. Hmph!" Shyne fussed and got frowned at by her mom and sister.

"They prove it when they get ghost when they can't get none. I'll just hold on to it until I meet the right guy," Christi to explained to nodding heads. "And no, I can't keep this handsome little fellow. I know someone in child services."

"OK. We'll make the call, so they can find him a good home. No more living in a cage for him," Shyne said nuzzling the baby's cheek.

"You are so, so, so very strange," Christi assured her little sister.

"She really is," Yolo cosigned. She grabbed the remote and turned the TV on and to the news.

'Breaking news! Social media star, Ashley Evens, was found dead in her Hollywood hills home...'

"Oh wow! That's where you guys were today!" Christi announced, pointing at the screen. Yolo and Shyne shared a quick glance and smirk. "I wonder what happened to her?"

'A confidential police source said she died from being asphyxiated by a sex toy.'

"Live by the sex toy, die by the sex toy," Shyne said and cracked up. "So, so very strange," Christi reiterated. The girls spent the night cooking and eating. In the morning, Christi reluctantly turned the child over to child services.

Chapter twenty seven

"Welcome home!" Asad grunted with the last few strokes that sent Shyne over the edge. She happily tumbled down 'orgasm hill' and landed in 'bust a nut' bliss.

"Mmm, you gonna make me leave again just so I can come back to this," Shyne purred like a kitty as her kitty throbbed happily.

"Well, you could go to the kitchen and come back. That would count," he said, ready for round two.

"Well, I will," she said, accepting the challenge.

She did and he fulfilled her desires. The couple copulated until they fell asleep in each other's arms. While Shyne was sleeping, her brother was busy creeping.

A local creep was preying on elderly victims in and around Atlanta with a scam. He made the mistake of calling the wrong elderly lady when he called Grandma Diedra.

"Diedra Forrest?" the scam artist inquired when he got the shrewd woman on the line.

"Yes?" she asked in reply with skepticism written on her pretty face. Only her grands and great grands ever called her phone, so she knew it was at least a wrong number. Hearing her name had her intrigued enough to play along since she had time to kill before Empire came on.

"Congratulations! You have been randomly selected to win an all expense paid cruise to the Bahamas!" he said and paused to let that sink in before he continued. "Seven nights and eight days, including port side excursions and all meals."

"Mm hm," Diedra hummed dubiously. She was old school and wise enough to know that scams only work on greedy people. People trying to get something for nothing and ending up with less than zero.

"All we need is your credit card information so we can secure your room," he said to seal the deal.

This was the same scam she just heard about ripping elderly people out of their dough. They fly down to the port of Miami only to find out there is no cruise, their credit cards ran dry and their identity stolen and maxed out.

"Well, I would love to go but..." she said and paused to set the hook in his mouth.

"But what, ma'am? It's a wonderful opportunity!" he stressed and prepared to hurdle any objection like an Olympic sprinter.

"It's just that I don't like to give my credit card information out over the phone. Is it possible that I can just meet you somewhere and just give the card to you? You can take it and do what needs to be done and just bring it back when you're finished."

"I..." he swooned as he thought of all the things he could do with the physical card. Numbers alone are golden to a thief, but the actually card was platinum. He would run a muck and run it up. Ironically, he was about to fall in the exact same trap he laid.

"Sure, sure! You can come to my room, um, the room the company provides when I'm in town."

"OK, give me the address and I'll be along in a little while," she said and took down his information. They said their goodbyes and terminated the call. "Xavier Sherrod Forrest!"

"Uh oh!" Yolo said when she heard his whole government name called.

"I know, right," he laughed and went to answer the summons. As he walked, he tried to recall what he could have done to get in trouble. A smile spread on his face when he determined he hadn't done a thing, so it must have been one of the kids. He was cool with that. "Sup ma?"

"My blood pressure. Some young man called, trying to get my credit card information for some so-called cruise around the world or some mess."

"I hope you didn't give it to them! It's a scam. They made off with millions of dollars last year," he explained.

"And they need dead for doing it. Taking advantage of elderly people like that," she whimpered softly. "And I agreed to meet him at his motel to give him my card."

"You're not meeting anyone, anywhere. What's his name and what's his address?" he demanded, extending his hand.

"Eric Estrada," she said and handed the handwritten information over. A sly smile spread on her face as Killa spun and marched away. She knew as surely as Monday follows Sunday, whoever he was, he was about to get fucked up.

"Baby I—" Killa began as he entered his room. Yolo was bucket naked on the bed with her face down and ass up and he forgot everything including his name and social security number.

"Yes?" she asked and gave her ass a wiggle. "Grandma OK?"

"Who? Oh yeah, I gotta call Sun," he said, coming closer to inspect the pretty pussy lips protruding from her thighs. He fondled them in one hand and used his phone with the other. Yolo soaked his fingers by the time Sun picked up. "It's so hot and wet!"

"What's hot and wet, pops?" Sun asked as he came on the line.

"Nothing you want to hear about," he assured him and relayed the information for the conman.

"Local or national news?" Sun asked so he would know how bad to do the man.

"Well, it was..." Killa began and paused to take a long lick like an ice cream cone. "It was your grandmother."

"So national? Say no mo'. Hello?" Sun asked when he realized he was on the phone alone. He had all he needed and set out to make headlines.

"You gotta go out. Family business," Bryonna mocked when her husband got off the phone.

"Yup, yup," he agreed, planting some parting kisses before he departed.

He gave her round belly a rub and kiss and set out to rid the planet of a bottom feeder who preyed on old folks. Sun's first stop was the stash house to chose a method of death. He fed the man-eating dogs in the yard and went inside.

"Let's see here," he said, twisting his lips in thought.

The family had amassed quite a few new devices for the upcoming clan rally. That made choosing all the more difficult. In the end, he settled on an old fashion, low-tech manner of death. He left the fancy devices and picked up a couple sets of plastic ties and a silencer-equipped pistol.

"Bad boys move in silence and violence," Sun rapped as he screwed the silencer on the gun. He drove over to the address and pulled into the motor lodge the conman called home. He switched motels on a regular basis to stay ahead of trouble, but this room would be his last because trouble just came a knocking.

"Diedra," Eric cheered and pumped his fist. He had big plans for her credit card and identity. He pulled the door open and flashed his bright smile. Sun flashed his gun causing his life to flash before his eyes.

"Back up," Sun barked and steered him back into his room. Eric flinched like he wanted to make a dash for it, so Sun silently sent a slug into his leg. He then lifted his own leg and shoved him back into the room.

"What? Who? How?" Eric pleaded, leaving out the why since he already knew. He knew his crimes would one day catch up to him and get him killed. The hole in his leg and man standing over him hinted that today was that day.

"Like you don't know. What you didn't know is you called the wrong grandmother," Sun growled and pressed the hot barrel to his forehead. It was going to leave a mark, but he wouldn't have to worry about it since the coroner would fix him up when they put him in a box.

"I'm sorry, bruh. I'll give her money back! Please don't shoot me bruh!" he moaned.

"I'm not. You have my word I'm not going to shoot you," Sun vowed as he cuffed his arms behind his back with the plastic ties. He secured his ankles next them bent his legs upwards and secured them to his arms.

"This is kinda uncomfortable," Eric advised.

"I'm sure, but it beats getting shot again, no?" Sun asked.

"Beats getting shot again, yes," he agreed. Sun stepped into the bathroom and turned on the water to fill the tub. "You taking a bath?"

"Nope, you are," he answered and began to drag him into the bathroom.

"Cuz, I'm dirty? No, cuz I do dirt? Dirty deeds?" he guessed as he got dragged. Sun ignored his questions, scooped him up and set him face down into the tub. Eric struggled and made some incomprehensible gargles as his lungs filled. Sun went to search the room for spoils of war. They had an unspoken rule that you got to keep whatever you find, but he forfeited the spoils in hopes some would go back to his victims.

Eric wasn't a fish, so the lungs full of water were sufficient for suffocation. Sun didn't even bother to check his pulse as he cut the ties off his wrist and ankles.

"A'ight, yo," Sun said over his shoulder as he left him face down in the tub.

*****

"A what!" Yolo shrieked when Sun filled her and Killa in on his latest kill.

"A Whitney. You know, face down in a bathtub, like Whit—" he began, but didn't get to finish.

"I get it and don't like it! I love Whitney Houston," Yolo pouted.

"Me either," Killa cosigned since she had a vagina. "How 'bout, um, a fish out of water?'"

"Un uh," Yolo shook her head. The room went silent as they brainstormed on a name for the manner of death.

"How about 'the mermaid'? Or in this case, 'merman,'" Shyne tossed out casually. She was slick hating since her brother got to do it first.

"I like it," Killa nodded. Yolo had no qualms, so it became law. "OK, that's settled. So, who's next?"

"We still have a couple of weeks until the jamboree," Yolo said and turned to the computer. She pulled up the 1-800-Killa site to read the request.

Chapter twenty eight

"Wait, you said what?" Yolo asked, cocking her head to make sure she heard her son correctly as he was recounting his visit to the con man.

"I said, 'A'ight, yo'. That's my new tag line. I hit 'em with it before I hit me with it," he explained. Mother Yolo looked dumbfounded while father Killa just shook his head.

"I don't know why you shaking your head. He get this corny mess from you!" she reminded.

"Got his good looks from me, too," he said.

He didn't deny being a nerd, though. He was, but was also the most dangerous man on the planet, so it balanced out.

"Anyway, good job, son. That dude was wanted in several states for bilking old folks out their dough. I would have sent a piece of him to every state too had it been me," Yolo bragged.

"Well, why don't you two handle this next one together?" Killa suggested. He turned to the laptop and read the next complaint to the 1-800-Killa site.

'Dear 1-800 Killa, my husband, my childrens' father, the love of my life was just killed for no reason. A bunch of badass kids threw a rock off the overpass and took him from us. The sheriff made a big production about bringing them to justice until he found out his own two sons were involved. Now its been swept under the rug and I have to look at these kids everyday.'

"Not any more, you don't," Yolo growled with a mouthful of malice.

"Why don't you take him with you?" Killa asked again.

"Him who?" she asked, looking for another him besides Sun.

She saw her son pout and gave in. "Oh ok."

"Gee, thanks, mom," he whined. He was actually thrilled to go make a kill with his legendary mother.

"And me and Shyne will take this next one," he said, turning back to the site and reading it.

'Dear 1-800 Killa, the police just killed my husband. To make matters worse he was a cop himself, a good cop who actually cared about his community. He was set to testify about some bad cops and they had him killed.'

"Yo, I remember that from the news!" Shyne said since it was local. "He got got the day before he was supposed to take the stand."

"And his brothers in blue had him whacked," Killa surmised.

"Should we put a lil' wager on this? See who gets most news coverage?" Yolo dared.

"The usual," Killa agreed. They always bet oral sex so the loser still won and the winner won big. A true win/win scenario.

"But of course," she said and fluttered her eyes seductively.

"Let's bounce," Sun said since he had his own wife to go home to. He wanted to spend some quality time inside her before he and his mother headed to Oklahoma to handle the rock throwing teens.

"Yeah!" Shyne fussed as if she was disgusted. Truth be told, she wanted to go home and hump her husband, as well. Everyone went to sex their spouse so they could set out and give some bad people what they need most dead.

*****

The family all met at the stash house to pick weapons for their missions. More like toys for their perspective play dates. Yolo and Sun had multiple targets, so they packed multiple guns and clips.

Killa and Shyne knew all roads led back to the precinct the cop worked in. A couple of crooked cops in cahoots with the local gang. The cops called the shots and the goons did the shooting.

"Be careful," Killa told his wife and son as they prepared to leave.

"OK," Yolo sang as she fluttered and fawned. She may have been a lunatic, but she was always giddy and girly around her husband. Their kids made faces, but they loved seeing their loving parents loving on each other.

"I'm driving," Sun said with a little extra bass in his voice indicating that he was in charge since his father wouldn't be there. He knew that men are the protectors and maintainers of women. All women.

"OK, baby," she said and let him take the wheel on every level. Killa and Yolo blew kisses at each other until they were out of sight. Once his wife was gone, he turned to his daughter.

"Well, lets drive by the west side and see what we can see," he suggested.

"Drive by or drive-by?" she asked, hoping for the latter.

"Reconnaissance," he said. "Once we see who the players are, we can do a drive-by."

"Yes!" she cheered and pumped her fist. The sweet girl always did love a good drive-by. Her father drove over to where the good cop was gunned down and took in the sights. They saw an unmarked police car pull up on a group of gang bangers who were obviously slanging.

"Hmmm," Killa wondered when no one ran. Instead, a tall lanky fellow walked to the driver and leaned in.

"Looks like he's the boss," Shyne said correctly.

"And the driver is the shot caller who got the cop shot," Killa added. They followed the cop car as she made several stops to drop off dope and pick up money. They confiscated drugs from other dealers and put them right back on the street. Now it was time to do a drive by.

*****

"Good timing," Yolo said when Sun pulled into town. She had pretended to be sleep most of the ride so he could speed in peace.

"Thanks, mom," he said and smiled. He may have grown to be a killer like his Killa dad, but was still a little boy, striving to please his mommy deep down inside.

"So, what's the plan?" she asked, allowing him to take the lead.

"My people got a lead on the kids. They are just kids, you know," he said in case she wanted to go easy on them.

"Man, fuck them kids!" she replied, meaning she did not. They were old enough to kill, so they were old enough to die. They decided to throw rocks at cars and now they were going to pay for it.

"Fuck 'em, then," Sun agreed and continued. "Most days, they'll all be in one of their houses playing video games.

"Shall we put some Sun-Shine in their lives?" she asked with glee as she produced her own.

"Wait, you got one, too?" he whined when he saw what was supposed to he his signature device.

"Yeah, well it's not like you got a patent on it," she shrugged. She ended up cracking up at the hurt look on his face.

"Anyway, let's slice and dice this kids into bite size pieces," he said and parked in front of the house. A quick head count said they were short two.

"The sheriffs' kids," Yolo surmised when she saw their car wasn't present. The sheriff decided to prosecute the other kids and spare his own, so he wouldn't let them hang out with them anymore.

"I'll go kick the door in and—" he began, but got cut off by his mother.

"You don't have to kick anything. They'll let me in. I'll leave the door open and you come in behind me," she said and got out. Sun watched curiously and wondered why the boys would let a strange woman into their house, especially an old grandmother like Yolo.

"Door!" Mickey fussed in reply to the chiming doorbell. It was his house, but since he and Johnny were on the game he ordered Mikey to get it.

"Probably Walter and William. Maybe daddy said they can come play with us again," Mikey said as he marched to the front door. He already had who it was in mind, so he snatched the door open. He saw the sexy lady and blinked in disbelief. The corny teens never had any girls come over so he was in shock.

"Hello," Yolo greeted and batted her eyes. Mikey grinned foolishly and a thin line of drool escaped his mouth.

"Who is it!" Mickey called from the rear.

"A milf!" he called back and snickered.

"I am a milf according to my husband," Yolo said and walked inside on him.

"A who? Whoa!" Mickey cheered and paused the game when he saw Yolo enter the den.

"A milf," she repeated for herself. She saw the excitement in their eyes turn to confusion when Sun walked in behind her.

"What's a milf, mom?" Sun asked, handing his mother her Sun-Shine.

"Ask him. He's the one that said it," she replied and all eyes shifted to Mikey.

"Um, like you know," Mikey stuttered and stammered as he shifted from foot to foot.

"Like a hot, like, older lady."

"You calling me old!" Yolo shrieked. Meanwhile, Sun pulled his phone and looked it up.

"Uh oh. According to this, you're a mom they'd like to fuck!" he said and hit the button. The nerds were in imminent danger, but had to marvel at the cool device.

Wow, he's got a light saber!" Johnny cheered and moved in for a closer look. Too close because two swipes of the super sharp, super heated blade chopped him into three pieces.

"I'm outta here!" Mickey announced and tried to make a run for it. Only problem was running requires legs and one swing of Yolo's blade removed both of his.

"Uh oh!" Mikey moaned and he was right. The mother and son moved on him together and made a mess of him. He was in 8 pieces by the time they were done.

"Three down, three to go," Yolo announced.

Sun did the math and realized she included the sheriff too for enabling his kids.

Chapter twenty nine

"Let's see your dad and sister top that!" Yolo proclaimed as she scanned the bloody room. They divided the three teens into eight different pieces and still had three more to go.

"I know, right?" he agreed and happily high-fived his mother. They left the crime scene and headed over to the sheriff's house to turn it into one, too. The sheriff was busy scolding his boys when they arrived to ruin their night.

"Why can't we hang out with our friends anymore!" Andrew pouted and stomped his foot. His whiny tone instantly grated Yolo's nerves.

"Ouch, why you pinch me?" Sun whispered when they witnessed the tantrum from a window.

"Cuz, you used to do that same thing. Ugh, can't stand a whiny boy," Yolo whispered back.

"Mom, focus," he said, shaking his head. They turned back to watch and await the chance to run in and kill them. Yolo and son left the machete in the car and brought other weapons of their destruction. She had a big ass gun while he brought a big ass rock. Not just any rock, thee rock.

"Because you fools keep doing stupid shit! How many times have I told you boys not to throw rocks at cars? Now you guys killed someone and I have to clean up the mess!" the father fussed. "Breaking into houses, stealing, using drugs, lying and now you actually killed someone!"

"And you are an enabler," Yolo said as she led the way inside. The sheriff immediately went for his gun on the table, but Yolo put a round right through his hand before he could pick it up.

"Yeeoow!" he screamed and looked clean through the hole in his hand.

"Who are you?" the boys asked her, but looked at the large rock Sun toted in behind her.

"Recognize it, huh?" Yolo said, reading their faces. "Yup, it's the same rock you threw through that man's window."

"He did it!" they both shouted and pointed at each other. They were both telling the truth since it was too heavy for either of them to lift by themselves. They both hefted it over the rail and tossed it down below and they were both about to pay for it.

"Who are you?" the sheriff asked once more and he put pressure on his wound to stop the bleeding.

"Someone who hates enablers," she replied and shot him again. This one was center mass and fatal. Four shots shredded his internal organs and left him fighting for his life. It was a fight he would not win.

"Lay down!" Sun barked at the teens. They both dropped face down and covered their heads. "Flip over."

"Like this?" the older brother asked just before Sun dropped the rock on his chest. The sound of ribs cracking reverberated in the room.

"Just like that," he said and picked up the rock. He slammed it back down and crushed his face.

"I'm outta here!" the surviving brother announced and hopped up to run. He hopped up, but Yolo gunned him back down. The wounds weren't fatal, but the subsequent rock attack was. The leg wounds dropped him to the floor and Sun stood over him and beat his head in with the same rock they used to kill the father.

"Yeah, let's see them top this!" Sun nodded and yet another brutal crime scene.

*****

"Did you see the news?" Shyne asked, sounding defeated when her dad came to pick her up.

"Don't be no punk," he advised. "It's good advice too that transfers to anything in life. No matter the obstacle or odds, trust God, go hard and don't be no punk."

"They sure made a mess of them dudes out there!" she sighed. "Chopped them into little pieces."

"Well, how about you do a little chopping of your own?" Killa suggested and flashed his Killer smile. Once they arrived at the stash house, he showed her what he had in mind.

"Oh, this will do some chopping," she exclaimed when he handed her an AK 47. They are affectionately known on the streets as choppers. The huge 7.62 rounds slice, dice and chop whatever they hit. They traded cars and rode across town to where the cops and robbers were one in the same. Killa parked where they could get a good view, but not be in view of all the cameras. They snarled as they watched the gang sling poison to their people like their ancestors fought for power to the people.

"Showtime!" Killa announced when he saw the unmarked police car creep up to the creeps. Shyne replied by sliding a round in the chamber. He stifled a chuckle at the murda mami scowl on her face. They both pulled their ski masks down and got down to business.

"Grrr," she growled as he crept forward. She waited until they were right on top of them before popping out of the sunroof like a Jack in the box. A Jack in the box is scary enough on its on, but when it has a chopper spitting flames, that's some extra scary shit.

"What the fu—" would be the cops final words as the big bullets began to shred the car.

The goon at the car did a full flip when the pounds touched his torso. The main cop saw a bullet rip through his partner's headrest and then head. He tried to duck in the car, but an A47 doesn't give a fuck about a car. He was soon as dead as his partner. Killa abandoned the drive-by when he saw a few thugs try to escape into the store. He put the car in park and went in after them while Shyne finished up outside.

"Over there!" the Chinese clerk said. pointing to where the thugs tried to hide.

She was tired of them running her customers off and stealing. They would never terrorize her family business again. Killa gave a gracious nod and walked to where she pointed. He went old school today and toted a throw back Mac-10 sub machine gun. The 45 caliber slugs squashed the thugs like bed bugs.

"Thank you," the clerk said with a slight bow and a candy bar to show her appreciation. Nothing says, 'thank you' for gunning down a bunch of low life thugs who terrorized our business like a Snickers bar.

"My pleasure," he nodded and accepted the tribute on his way out. Shyne had gotten out too to make sure not one of them survived. They made eye contact, signaling it was time to go.

"I got six," Shyne bragged as they pulled away from the crime scene.

"There was eleven inside," Killa replied. He seen his daughter's lip twist like 'yeah right' and came clean. "OK, three."

"For a total of nine!" she cheered since the score was 6 for Yolo and Sun and 9 for the father/daughter duo.

A smile spread on Killa's face on winning the bet. He would have enjoyed paying up if he lost, but winning felt so much better. Shyne smiled too seeing the smile on her father's face. They rode over to the stash spot to stash the guns, switch cars and head home.

"You ready for the main event baby girl?" Killa asked purely for conversation since he knew his baby girl stayed ready. They all had been counting down the days to the jamboree like Christmas.

"Hells—I mean, heck yeah!" she shot back. Little black kids were still going missing and they all knew the answer would be found at the WLM rally. They had no idea how right they were. They weren't the only ones preparing for the big event.

*****

"This will be our best jamboree yet!" Jeffrey, the reigning Grand Puba bragged to the woman below.

"Mmhm," she hummed and nodded since her mouth was full. Actually, half full since he didn't have enough dick to fill a whole mouth. Either way, she was paid to suck dick, not talk.

"We got over two thousand brothers and sisters coming! We have all kinds of games and activities," he rambled, while she worked her head, neck and lips quickly so he could get off and she could get up and get out.

"Mmhm," she repeated and worked. Brenda couldn't stand the racist redneck with the little pink dick. He was always 'nigga this and nigga that' as if she was an inanimate object. A throwback to when master would talk in front of the slaves like they didn't exist.

"We got pin the tail on the nigga. Monkey see, monkey do. Bobbing for nigga. Black face rap contest. Gonna auction off a hundred little nigga babies! Nigga this, nigga that..." he went on and on until interrupted by busting a nut.Brenda pulled away to cheat him out of one the best parts a blow job, the beginning and the end. She denied him a warm, wet place to skeet and stood to leave.

"Well, I would invite you to the jamboree but, you're black," he laughed as if she was supposed to laugh along with him. "If I did, I'd have to sell you."

"Whatever, honky. Just give me my bread," she insisted. He pouted at her tone, but broke bread.

"Next time?" he asked hopefully. His puritanical wife scoffed at sucking dick, so he headed over to the hood for head.

"Next time, suck yo' own damn dick!" she spat figuratively, then literally and spit at feet. All money ain't good money and this money was the worse. She balled the bills up and tossed them over her shoulder in the motel parking lot as she left. She had no idea her words would one day come true.

*****

"Yeah, yeah. You won. A bet is a bet," Yolo sighed and began her descent down Killa's torso. She was fronting though because pleasing her man was one of her biggest pleasures.

"It is," Killa agreed as she kissed her way down south. She stopped to kiss and suck his Adam's apple then down to his chest. "Mmmm."

The couple locked eyes as she slid her mouth over his head like a snake swallowing its prey. Neither blinked as she eased him into her mouth. A slight gag indicated when she couldn't take no more. Had the staring been a contest, Killa lost when she twirled her tongue over the head and made his eyes roll back in his head.

"Technically, it was a tie," Killa proclaimed and pulled his wife around into a 69. He held out as long as he could until Yolo howled in delight. Once he got her off, he rolled her off and flipped her onto her back.

"I'm so in love with you," she admitted as he wriggled inside of her.

"Mmhm," he nodded since this was no time to talk. The look in his eyes relayed it anyway as he searched for and found his stroke. And stroke he did. Killa hit it from the front then flipped her on her side. He hit it from the side then flipped her on her belly. He hit her face down, ass up, then pulled her onto her hands and knees for classic back shots. The inevitable drew near, so he flipped her back onto her back so he could fuck her face to face.

"Come on, baby," she purred and stroked his back. Killa couldn't hold out any longer and exploded with a roar. Yolo held him and rubbed his back as he writhed in pleasure. Soft kisses signaled the end of the episode.

"I'm in love with you, too," he said as he pulled out and rolled off onto his back. Yolo scurried over and snuggled up on his chest. Snores soon filled the room.

Chapter thirty

"Yeee Haa!" Camiesha screamed and threw her hips into overdrive. Her wild cowboy routine was always a wild ride, but today it was a little extra. She threw one hand in the air and spun her hips while riding the dick. Trigga was blind, but could see something was up. Now wasn't the time to bring it up since she was bouncing and winding her hips on his dick. No, this is no time for questions. This was time to grip hips and hold on. "Yeee Haa!"

Camiesha felt the explosion building to the point of no return. She flexed her vaginal muscles and gripped the wood inside of her with all she had. All those Kegel exercises paid off because she pulled Trigga over the edge with her. They both seized and shook from the strong orgasm until it subsided. Camiesha turned around to cuddle with her man and bask in the after glow of a good, good nut.

"You OK? Your heart is beating so hard. I ain't fuck you to death, did I?" Camiesha bragged like a person does when they know they just rocked the house.

"I'm good. Sup with you, tho? What you got going on?" Trigga asked. He leaned up and faced her as if looking at her. He didn't need to see her to know what she did. "Don't twist your lips up at me, shawty."

"How you—" she asked, waving her hand in front of his blind eyes. "Me? Nothing? Why you ask? Me? Un-uh, not up to nothing. Not me, un-uh."

Now it was Trigga's turn to twist his face up dubiously. Their sex life was vibrant and vigorous, but lately it had been extra. Extra head, extra back shots and extra wild cowgirl rides.

"Oh, OK!" Camiesha fussed and began to confess. She was in love and lying is not a part of love. "You know I have to go stateside next week, right?"

"Yeah, family reunion, business," he replied. They agreed he would stay home and take care of their son.

197

"Well, I'm gonna stop by and see Rude Boy," she admitted and braced herself for his reaction.

"Glad you decided to tell me. I kinda figured you would," he replied. He knew she was a dope girl to her heart and couldn't help herself. They lived very comfortably, so it wasn't about the money, but the thrill. He wasn't able to provide good advice because he was a dope boy to his heart. He dreamed of being back in the hood. Blunt in mouth, pistol in pants, slinging rocks to junkies and dodging po-po.

"I can't help it," she admitted with the anguish of a junkie. This was her one last hit before rehab, just like a junkie.

"I know, but yo' pops gone lose his mind!" Trigga warned. Cam was a street legend in his eyes, so his word held weight.

"No, he not cuz he ain't gone know. If he ask you anything, just say you didn't see me do anything," she said and cracked a smirk.

"You got jokes, huh," Trigga said, twisting his lips. He never let on how much her blind jokes bothered him since he knew she meant no harm.

"I'm sorry, baby. You know I love you," she purred and planted apologetic kisses all over his face. "Real talk, baby. Just one lick. One time and I'm done."

"Babe, that's some bullshit. We got plenty of bread. We straight and you wanna risk it all, for what?"

Camiesha pressed her lips together to prevent something sarcastic from slipping out. She shrugged her shoulders since she didn't have a good explanation. Belize was quiet, slow and safe and she needed some excitement. Trigga rolled off the bed and went to shower the sex away.

*****

"Does your father know about this?" Rude Boy asked when Camiesha came to make a buy.

"Um, one, I'm grown and two, it's my money," she said, speaking his language.

"So, three bricks, huh?" he asked and nodded at the extra 18 grand he was about to make. "Yo, you got a way in, right? You can't just carry this shit in your carryon you know?"

"Bruh, do I look crazy to you?" she dared, twisting her lips and cocking her head.

"Nah, you look sexy. When you gonna come hang out with me?" he cracked for a hundredth time.

"And do what?" she asked and bit her bottom lip. She twirled her finger around her curls and batted her big brown eyes.

"Whatever you wanna do. I own a hotel. Pick a room," he advised. "Been wanting to suck on that fat poom-poom."

'You can, but I just fucked my man and it's full of cum," she smiled and continued twisting her hair.

"I'll take a rain check," he grimaced at the thought.

"Nah, you won't. So let me get that work," she said, getting back to business. Rude Boy let out a deep sigh and stood. He was obviously excited at the prospect of bedding the sexy young woman and hand a bulge in his pants. He locked eyes with Camiesha as he adjusted as if to say 'see what you're missing'. She had plenty dick at home, so she turned her head.

A few minutes later, Rude Boy returned with a bag containing the three bricks. She pulled stacks of cash from her purse and counted out the eighteen thousand dollars and placed it on his desk.

"I hope you know what you're doing," he warned affectionately and handed over the bag.

"I got this, yo," she assured him, minus the eye contact that should accompany an assurance. She almost ducked as she collected the bricks and slinked out of the office. Rude Boy zoomed in on the booty until she reached her truck and pulled away.

"I hope you know what you're doing," he repeated to her wake.

*****

"We meet again," Killa told his cousin and they gave a pound and hug.

"Killa/Cam ride again!" Cam cheered as they embraced. "Ride with me out to the airport so I can pick up Camiesha."

"Bet," he agreed and followed him out to his new Mercedes. "Nice whip."

"Thanks, it's my wife's. You know I'm low-key now and push a pick-up truck," Cam replied.

He and his wife bought a few acres out in the sticks where he raised a few chicken and sheep. He wouldn't be the last dope boy to turn farmer. The cousins chatted it up as they rode down to Hartsfield International airport. Camiesha's flight was about to land and she was sweating bullets.

"Shit!" Camiesha cursed herself and her reckless decision to carry coke in her carryon bag. She didn't even have time to try to disguise it. Three perfect bricks of pure cocaine were wedged between her dainty panties and bras. She had no idea on who she would use to move the work since Self and Bad was were living in Houston.

"Are you OK?" the nerdy guy seated next to her asked. He had been trying to figure out a way to talk to the pretty young lady the entire trip. The stewardess had just announced fasten seat belts for descent so it was now or never.

"Mind your—" Camiesha started to snap, but caught herself. "I mean, no. I'm not feeling well. Can I rest my head on your shoulder?"

"Yes!" he shouted, drawing attention. Camiesha flashed her sweet smile and laid her head on his shoulder. She reached for his clammy hand and held it until they landed and taxied to the terminal.

"Let me!" the nerd pleaded when Camiesha reached overhead for her bag and was wracked by a phantom pain.

"Thank you," she fawned, batted her eyes and took off. The nerd had to walk briskly to keep up with Camiesha as she sped towards the baggage claim area. He caught up with her on the moving sidewalk, but she still distanced herself from him and wouldn't look at him.

"There she is!" Killa pointed when he spotted her first. Cam was looking towards the tram thinking she would have taken it.

"Meet me at the carousel," she told the nerd over her shoulder and ran into Cameron's open arms. "Hey, daddy!"

"Hey, sweetheart. How are you?" he asked and squeezed.

"I'm fine," she replied as they pulled away to look at each other then hugged once again.

"Sup yo," Killa greeted and hugged his niece. The two of them had put in some work together once or twice and had history.

"Chillin', yo!" she shot back in her mock New York accent. The girl now added a Belizian patois to her repertoire of dialects. She was fluent in South Bronx slang, ATL twang, Mississippi swag and now Central American drag.

"Let's get your bags and get up out of here," Cam said since the airport was one of his least favorite places. It was swarming with several types of law enforcement personal and made him uneasy.

"Hey, I—" the nerd said when Camiesha came over to collect her bag from the carousel. She screwed her face up and turned away. She spotted her bag and pointed it out to her dad.

"What the—ugh, did you pack?" Cam grunted as he snatched the moving bag from the carousel and almost got pulled on.

"Just clothes," she replied, not revealing they were revealing club clothes since she planned to party. She planned to shop too which made the extra clothes futile, but that's Camiesha.

"Here, I have to go," the nerd whined and gave her the carryon bag. Camiesha did a quick scan before she accepted it.

"No, you didn't! Tell me you didn't!" Cam fussed, while Killa frowned curiously.

"What she do?" Killa asked, trying to figure out what he missed. He had to trot to keep up with Cam as he rushed to the parked car.

"I couldn't help it, daddy. I'm sick. I need help!" she pouted. He ignored her until they reached his car and pulled out of the parking lot.

Once they reached the highway, he looked at through the rear view and let her have it.

"Girl, what the hell is wrong with you? Why in the world would you bring blow in the first place! And in your carryon!"

"I—"

"Shut up. Just be quiet," he fussed. Camiesha knew she fucked up, crossing her arms over her chest and sticking her bottom lip out. She rode like that for the rest of the ride.

"Well, handle your business and be ready to ride by Wednesday. The rally is this weekend," Killa announced when they arrived at Cam's house. Camiesha was still pouting.

"Bye, unc," she said and gave him a hug. She had to grab her own suitcase from the truck and drag it into the house.

"Nice to see you again!" Michelle sang and wrapped Camiesha up into her arms. She twisted her lips curiously, seeing her husband with the small bag and her dragging the heavier one. She looked between them and shrugged. By now, she knew and accepted she married into a family of weirdos. It was all good since some of the best singers, artist and authors are oddballs. "Welp, I 'm off to bed. See you guys in the AM."

"Good night," Cam and Camiesha sang like a choir, causing her to twist her lips once more. They pasted smiles on their faces until she disappeared up the winding staircase.

"So, you gonna flush it down the toilet?" Camiesha moaned at the loss of her 18 grand.

"Flush? Nah, we 'bout to cook this shit up! Bet a stack my whip game is better than yours!"

"Pops, I will drag you!" she shot back, accepting the challenge. Luckily, Michelle was a sound sleeper because she would have lost her whole mind had she came down and caught them cooking coke in her good pots.

Chapter thirty one

"Is this everything you need, grandma?" Killa asked as he delivered Diedra's shopping list. Some of the items had to be secured through his network since sodium cyanide wasn't on supermarket shelves along with the Country Time lemonade.

"Let's see," she said, donning rubber gloves and gas mask. Killa blinked in disbelief since he just transported all that stuff in his vehicle. "Looks like it's all here. Enough to cook for two thousand."

"Cool. I'll have it shipped out to Yellowstone," he said since he would not be transporting it again. He and Sun were tasked with driving a rental truck filled with the tools of their trade. The rest of the family would fly out and set up camp ahead of the white supremacist.

"Is my grandbaby on the way?" Diedra asked. She was surrounded by her other great grands, but always missed her Camiesha.

"Yeah, Cam said they had to make a stop out in Decatur and would be here right after," he replied and donned her mask to take the poison back out of the house.

"Wonder what they're doing in Decatur?" the nosey woman wondered aloud.

"Hmph," Killa huffed, meaning he knew but wasn't telling.

*****

"For real, daddy? You really gonna do this? Like for real, for real?" Camiesha pleaded as her dope boy daddy drove towards Decatur.

He replied in the affirmative when he pulled off I-20 on Candler road. A quick turn later and they were heading down the hill in the sprawling Eastwyck apartment complex.

Her head turned towards the apartment they once used to stash their work. She saw familiar faces as they neared the trap. Some were still trapping while a few were now smokers. The hood is like a hungry monster that chews up the weak and shits them back out as junkies. It now kinda made sense why he was doing what he was doing. Almost, but she was still out 18 grand.

Cameron parked and walked over to an apartment of one his original crew. Sammy was born here and planned to die here. His old school bubble Chevy still sat in the parking lot as a reminder of days gone by.

"Ca—Cameron Forrest? Is that you!" he screamed and snatched him off his feet in an embrace. The merriment died when Camiesha walked in behind him. He recalled the wicked young woman during her short reign over the trap. "What's she doing here?"

"She's my daughter," Cam explained and frowned to match his frown.

"She must be adopted cuz—hmph!" he huffed at her. Cameron turned and raised an eyebrow for explanation.

"I wouldn't let them eat when I was out here. I was tryna run the check up..." she said and trailed off.

"And she wants to make up for it now. Don't you sweetheart?" he insisted.

"Yeah," she said and twisted her highly glossed lips. That was Cam's cue to produce 4.4 pounds of cooked coke.

"For me?" the old hustler asked and teared up. Slinging dope is a young man's game and the old timer had been squeezed out. Now, all he had were war stories to reminisce over.

"For you," Cameron nodded and officially made him the plug. Camiesha won the coke cookoff, but they produced a little over 5 bricks of primo crack from the three original keys. Sammy got 2 of them and Cam distributed the other amongst his other old friends.

"Feel better?" she asked sarcastically after they gave away the last of the blow.

"Yup, you?" he laughed at her tone and screwed up face.

"Actually yeah, I do, cuz them dudes stuck. They ain't never gonna go nowhere or do nothing," she admitted. "But still, I'm out 18 racks."

"Yeah? Well lessons costs," he chuckled and steered the car towards cousin Killa's house. "Tuition."

*****

"Camiesha!" Diedra screeched when her beloved entered the house.

"Oh shit," Camiesha muttered when she realized the old lady got the drop on her. She didn't have time to properly prepare for a 'grandma hug'. Those things can be lethal if not ready. Children have been snapped in half by 'grandma hugs'.

"She dying," little Killa said, removed his fitted cap and placed it over his heart. He lowered his head as Camiesha's eyes rolled in her head when she neared unconsciousness. Grandmas obviously have some sort of meter because Diedra let her go just in the nick of time.

"How's my baby? And where's my baby?" she asked, looking around for Camiesha's son.

"He stayed in Central America with his dad," she replied. leaving out the part of wanting a break so she could turn up. She lost her shopping money, but still had plenty of turn up clothes in her suitcase.

"I see," she said since she was a professional at reading between the lines.

"Well, I gotta pick up X from the airport. Rico is supposed to be on his way," Killa relayed.

"Sun and Bryonna just pulled up and Shyne and Asad should be here soon," Yolo said, accounting for the entire Killa clan. That meant the WLM movement was about to come to a screeching halt.

"Yo, tell em," little Killa urged to his spokemen. Yolo let out a deep sigh when little Diedra stepped up to speak. She put her hand on her little hip and tapped her foot waiting for family banter to subside so she wouldn't have to repeat herself.

"We're staying here. My brother and I decided we don't want to go camping. He won't be able to play his games and I need mirrors and hair products. So..." she tailed off and rolled her eyes.

"Girl stop!" grandma guffawed and set off a round of laughter. Diedra and Killa got laughed out of the room. They stomped off with pouty faces and potty mouths.

"This some real bullshit," little Killa fussed. Lucky for him, his mother didn't hear him over all the laughter.

Once the entire family was assembled, big Killa did his thing on the grill surrounded by his sons, son-in-law and grandson. The women folk congregated in the den for their last meal before the big trip. Killa booked rooms and tents in Yellowstone so they could strike.

*****

"I'll see you boys in a few," Killa said as Xavier and Rico loaded up into a rental truck. They planned to pull out all the stops, so they brought the entire arsenal, including Sun killer canines.

"A'ight, pops," they said and pulled off. He almost wished he were riding with them instead of the luxury RV Yolo decided to rent at the last moment. That meant he had to drive with his lunatic family. Shyne, Asad, Sun and Bryonna drove another SUV for the convo out west

"Oh, come on, punk," Yolo teased when he came home moping. He looked at the massive vehicle and sighed once more. It was already rocking from the activities inside.

"I got your punk," he mumbled and boarded the bus size vehicle.

"Don't worry. I'm gonna ride shotgun with you. And as soon as everyone goes to sleep, I'm gonna give you the best blow job of your life!" she vowed.

"OK, all aboard! Let's get this show on the road!" he barked and jumped behind the wheel. Nothing motivates a man like good head. "Every one move! Let's get in gear! Move it! Move it!"

Yolo kept her word several times over the 3-day drive. Sun and Asad took turns driving, but neither got the same motivation as dear old dad. Little Killa was calm since the luxury rig had several TVs for him to play his games. They arrived at Yellowstone national park in the middle of the night. Killa snuck his wife off to one of the reserved rooms for a good sleep and privacy. They were two days ahead of the rally, which gave them time to set up.

"We need to kill every one of them," Yolo announced as they lay in bed the next morning.

"If we don't, they'll just regroup and be right back at it," he agreed. Killing two thousand people at once was easier said than done. That's why they brought the whole clan.

"Welp, let me get some before them people come for breakfast," Yolo said, reaching for his crotch.

"You are so romantic," Killa quipped as he got groped. His body didn't know the difference and soon she held a full-fledged erection in her hand. Yolo debated on whether to ride it forward or backwards and decided to go forward.

"Cuz, you so pretty," she said, explaining her choice to ride him face to face. He replied by gripping her ass and guiding her up and down on his dick. He was an excellent driver and steered them both to a mutual orgasm just in time before the family arrived at the hotel. They showered, dressed and met them down in the dining room.

"Hmph, someone got a glow to their face. No wonder you left us on that greyhound," Diedra huffed when Killa and Yolo joined them.

"Grandma, that's a two hundred thousand dollar rig!" Killa reeled.

"Mmhm," she replied, meaning she was done with it. They ordered, ate and got busy getting ready for the big day.

******

"So, run in and murder everything moving?" Camiesha asked as Yolo parked across the street from a catering service. They got the call to provide meals for the WLM rally. Even Yolo frowned at the brutal suggestion, but it answered the questions she had about the woman.

"Or not," Diedra fussed and shook her head. "We just need to get into the kitchen."

"Oh, I know! My girl Dre told me how her man Ra infiltrated a spot and..." Camiesha said and filled them in.

"Well, we don't have to shoot her," Yolo said when the middle-aged baker left for lunch. That left a young, pimple-faced teen holding down the fort. "You think you can distract him enough for us to get into the back?"

"You think I can't?" Camiesha shot back and undid the top buttons of her blouse. She pushed her push up bra making her ta-tas poke out.

"Camiesha!" Diedra fussed, then hushed since they were on a mission. Camiesha got out and sashayed into the catering office.

"Can I—oh my!" pimple boy reeled when he saw sexy Camiesha enter the store. He had been trained on what to say when manning the shop by himself, but couldn't remember a word of it.

"Do you guys do baby showers?" Camiesha asked as he practically drooled on her cleavage.

"Huh? Oh yeah, but you have to wait 'til Mrs. Bridges gets back from lunch. I can—"

"Well, show me your cake catalog," she said, steering him away as Diedra entered the shop. He tried to turn his head to the door, but she wouldn't let him. A shimmy of her shoulders shook her caramel breast and stole his attention once more.

"Let's see here," Diedra said, looking around. A large pot labeled WLM caught her eye and she wandered over to it. She quickly dumped a bottle of sodium cyanide into the BBQ sauce. "Now, it's spicy!"

"OK, well thank you," Camiesha said abruptly once her grandmother eased back by. Her work was done and now it was time for the rest of the family to put in work.

Chapter thirty two

"Here's the plan," Killa began once he had all the players in place. Sun and Shyne had to sneak out on their sleeping spouses to attend the late night briefing. Grandma's work was done, so she stayed back at the hotel.

"Kill them all!" Shyne interrupted and got shut down by a glance from her dad. "My bad."

"Yes, baby. Kill them all. Yolo, Shyne, and Camiesha will post out in snipers nest here, here and here," he said, pointing out there positions on the Google earth display.

"Anyone runs, gets gunned."

"But errbody gonna have on hoods. How we gonna make sure we don't shoot you guys?" Camiesha moaned.

"With this," Yolo answered and handed her a pair a goggles. "Look at their robe and hood."

Oh! Cool!" she replied when the guys' disguises had a green glow with the glasses.

"Way cool. Still we'll be coming out the robes once the shooting starts," Killa corrected and continued. "Rico and X will be on stage performing in black face."

"With choppers under our robes," Xavier snarled. He may not have shared the same DNA as Killa, but he was Killa's son all day long. They would bring the killer pooches on stage with them. They had been trained to attack the white robes for the last few weeks.

"And these, everyone will have one of these," Killa said, holding up the Sun-Shine machete.

"Awe man! Everyone gets my thing!" Sun pouted and got laughed at.

"Told you to get a patent," Yolo snickered. A stern look from Killa shut her down, too. It didn't prevent her from sticking her tongue out at him when he turned back to the display.

"I saw that. Anyway, Sun, Cousin Cam and I will mix in with the people. Once X gives the signal, we set if off!" he wrapped up. The three infiltrators would all carry fully automatic H&K MP-5 sub machine guns and extra clips.

"Oh, one last thing. Do not eat anything. Especially the BBQ!" Yolo warned.

"I love BBQ! My grandma said she made it!" Rico cheered. This was the same child who ate poisoned peanuts his mother once set out for the mice. Even after being told nine times they were poisoned peanuts for the mice.

"Yeah and she put cyanide in it, so," Yolo said and was done with it.

"So, I probably shouldn't eat it, huh?" he asked with a curious frown.

"You can have a little," Killa said, shaking his head. "Anyway, this is Jeffrey. He is the reigning Grand Puba. I got ten thousand for his head."

"I'm gonna buy Bryonna something really nice with that ten grand," Sun nodded approvingly.

"That's nice except I'm getting that money," Shyne shot back. She didn't need it, but she was just competitive like that.

"Studio time," Xavier said, announcing his plans for the money. Rico chimed in next as Yolo and Killa smiled at each other at what he had started. It didn't matter who got Jeffrey, but Jeffrey was definitely getting got.

*****

"What do we have here?" Jeffrey asked as he opened a large shipping container at the campground. The hundred black kids inside cowered and blinked from the sudden light.

"You little niggas hungry?"

"I was just about to feed them," the guard announced in reply.

"Good, cuz no one wants to buy a skinny little nigga," he nodded approvingly and turned to leave. "Oh, no BBQ for them!"

"That's 'whites only' BBQ," the guard laughed and rubbed his hands together in anticipation.

He wouldn't have to wait long because the festivities were about to begin.Jeffrey made his rounds and made sure everything was all set as the campground began to fill up. Redneck of every state, occupation, and background converged on the campsite. There were both blue and white collars rednecks with one thing in common. A sick, twisted hatred of all things and people nonwhite.

The Killa women surrounded the rally and get a watchful eye through the scope their high-powered rifles. Killa and Sun dressed in the WLM knockoff KKK robes. Gloves covered caramel-colored hands while shades hid brown eyes behind dark glass. X and Rico got the giggles as they dressed in black face for their performance. Seems the rednecks like rap music. Go figure.

"What the heck is that, pops?" Sun asked in awe as Killa added a final prop to his costume.

"A sickle, except it does this,"Killa said and hit the switch. He chuckled when Sun's eyes lit up along with the blade. "The sickle of death."

"Yooo! That's dope! I want one!" he insisted, but no such luck.

"No can do. I got it patented," he said with a smirk and pulled his hood on.

"That's that bull shi—anyway, you look like the grim reaper!" Sun cheered. He always was and always would view his father as a superhero.

"Yeah well, I am Killa."

*****

"Shooter 1 set," Yolo announced into her walkie-talkie followed by shooters 2 and 3 when Shyne and Camiesha checked in. Everyone had earpieces in to communicate discreetly.

"Black and Sambo set," Rico reported once he and his brother were back stage.

Both had disguised their melanin with black face make up and gloves. Both had fully automatic weapons under their robes and a dog on a leash. The dangerous dogs were agitated by all the white robes. They growled and slobbered in anticipation of eating some white meat.

"Black Sambo," Killa repeated, shaking his head. "Anyway, the food just arrived and the first act just took the stage."

"No survivors!" Shyne snarled through her radio and set the tone. The rest of the family echoed her sentiments in unison. "No survivors!"

A hard rock band took the stage first doing their smash hit, Jigga-boo. Throngs of people lined up to get plates of poisoned ribs, pulled pork and chicken. Every bite represented one less bullet they had to fire. Yolo watched a couple sneak off from their spouses and creep into the woods.

"Just messy," Yolo fussed as she saw the adulterous act unfold.

"Hurry up!" the blonde said and pulled her jeans down. She bent over and leaned against a tree to brace for back shots.

"Won't take me but a few minutes," he assured her as he entered. Being a minuteman comes in handy at times like this, but he didn't even last a whole minute. Yolo closed one eye, held her breath and aimed at his Modula oblongata. A squeeze of the trigger sent a silent slug that turned off his lights instantly.

"Already? I could have stay with Billy Bob for that!" she complained when he fell out of her and away. She spun and leaned down to see blood and brain matter everywhere. Instinctively, she looked around for her jealous husband. "Billy Bob?"

"OK, bye-bye," Yolo sang happily and fired another round. Rumors of her being an airhead were proved untrue when her brains splattered against the tree.

"Nice shot, mom," Shyne congratulated. She had taken aim on the couple of cheaters herself, but her mother beat her to the punch.

"Thanks. Take a look at their spouses they snuck off from!" she replied. Shyne and Camiesha both trained their sights on Billy Bob and the other woman as they snuck off to do the do, as well.

"I want one!" Camiesha whined.

"I'll take him. You can have her," Shyne said graciously. It's always nice when family can share.

"Cool," she said and took aim at his ten gallon hat. They watched as the woman kneeled and removed Billy's Bob from his jeans. She leaned in and took him down her throat. It had all the slobbery goodness of a good blowjob, but it was about to be cut short.

'Psst' the two sniper rifles whispered in unison and sent large projectiles tumbling towards their targets. Camiesha didn't plan on a trick shot, but her round went through the woman's head while giving head and hit Billy's Bob in its head. He opened his mouth to let out a scream, but Shyne's bullet sped in and shut him up. It knocked his brain out the back of his head and onto the leaves below.

"OK, you guys. Stop playing around. It's showtime," Killa said as the rock band rapped up their insulting set. People were starting to nod off from the all around the campground. They drifted off to dead and would wake up on the other side in the afterlife.

"That was the Alt-right doing their smash hit, Jiggaboo! Give them another round of applause!" Jeffrey announced as he took the stage. The dwindling crowd all clapped and cheered in response. "I see some of you are getting sleepy, so we'll have the auction after this next act. I hope you brought plenty of cash so you can take a little nigga home with you. Speaking of nigga, this next act... Surprise honkies? What a name. Anyway, give it up for surprise honkies!"

"Lets get it!" X growled and led his brother on stage. The large dogs were in a frenzy when they saw the sea of white robes and hoods.

"Let's," Rico said with a sinister smile. Both had their guns locked and loaded under their robes ready to rip. They scanned the crowd through their filtered glasses and easily spotted their family members.

"What's up, you red neck no good crackers!" X called into the mic and got the crowed hyped. The erupting crowd agitated the dogs even more.

"Surprise Honkies!" Rico said and released his dog. Xavier did too and they attacked the closest red necks.

They grabbed them by their red necks and snatched their throats out. The stunned crowd froze in place unsure if it was a part of the act or not. The screams and blood seemed real enough, but when the robes came off and the choppers came out there was no mistaking what was happening. X and Rico upped the machine guns and sprayed the crowd like they were watering the grass. Killa and Cam pulled off their robes too, so they wouldn't get shot.Or worse, bit by one of those big ass dogs.

The crowd tried to escape to the left, but there was Killa spitting fire out of his own chopper. They tried to go right, but there was Cousin Cam. Sun brought up the rear and there was nowhere to go except dead. The ladies didn't have the patience to wait on runners and picked off people from their post. Not just impatience, killing racist is always a lot of fun. So much fun it should be an Olympic sport.

Jeffrey realized there was no escape, so he ran towards the containers holding the slaves. At least he would have something to bargain with he thought. By the time the shooting stopped, gun smoke wafted into the night air. It looked like a smolderingforest fire, but in truth, it was a Forrest family fire.

The patriarch scanned the ground and saw there were quite a few hardheaded people who hadn't died yet.

"Lets give them some Sun-shine shall we?" he announced.

Accordingly, everyone pulled their blades and turned them on. He hit the switch on his sickel and they murdered them.

"Now, for ole Jeffrey!" Killa said, rubbing his hands together in anticipation as he led the way over to the shipping container.

"Dang!" Camiesha exclaimed when he pulled the door open and they saw the black babies stuffed inside like a slave ship. "Grrrr!"

"Help! I saved them! I found all these missing children!" Jeffrey proclaimed, trying his luck. And why wouldn't he after the massacre he just witnessed.

"He's funny!" Yolo cracked up. She turned to Camiesha who was emitting a low, guttural growl with her pretty face balled into a mask of murder. "Get him, lil' mama."

"Ten bands on his head," Shyne dared charitably. None of them needed the money, but they all wanted the honor of ending his dishonorable life. Everyone turned their blades off to let Camiesha have him.

"Not in front of the kids. Drag him outside," Killa directed and his three sons immediately carried it and him out.

"But wait, I saved them!" Jeffrey pleaded as he was dragged outside. Yolo and Shyne stayed to check on the children and missed the main event.

"Save this!" Camiesha grunted and took both legs off, below the knee with one swipe of the super heated blade. He let out a blood-curdling howl that made the wolves in the woods holler back. Jeffrey raised an arm to deflect the next blow and lost it. He did it again and lost the other one.

"Uh oh!" Xavier grimaced when Camiesha snatched his pants down. Meanwhile, Rico locked in on her booty since she wasn't blood and she was turning him on.

"Ouch!" the five men groaned and grabbed their junk when she cut his off.

"Shut up all that noise!" she demanded and stuffed his jewels in his mouth. The family stood over the racist as his life's blood leaked onto the earth and he choked on his chicken. Smiles spread on all faces when the rattle of death emitted from his throat as his soul departed for judgment.

"What we gone do with them?" Yolo asked. hooking a finger towards the container full of children. It was too many to take with them and they certainly couldn't be there when the cops came knocking.

"Use his phone," he replied nodding his head at the Jeffrey pieces scattered about. She found his phone and made the cryptic call to 911. She sat the phone down, but left it on so authorities could trace the phone. "Let's bounce."

The Forrest family turned and walked back through the woods to where they peaked and departed the worse crime scene in history. It was one heck of a family reunion.

The End

www.ingramcontent.com/pod-product-compliance
Lightning Source LLC
Chambersburg PA
CBHW011503170626
46812CB00008B/2957